NEVER A MERE MORTAL

ISBN: 979-8-9852230-0-2 (Paperback)
        979-8-9852230-2-6 (Hardcover)

Library of Congress Control Number: 2021922893

This is a work of fiction and any resemblance to real places or persons, living or dead, is purely coincidental. Names, characters, and places are products of the author's imagination.

First published in Huntsville, Alabama.

Cover art and illustration by Dial Design Studio.

*For the bride of Christ –
may we fall deeper
in love with the Groom,
that they may know us by our love.*

"It is a serious thing to live in a society of possible gods and goddesses, to remember that the dullest and most uninteresting person you talk to may one day be a creature which, if you saw it now, you would be strongly tempted to worship, or else a horror and a corruption such as you now meet, if at all, only in a nightmare. All day long we are, in some degree, helping each other to one or other of these destinations…There are no ordinary people. You have never talked to a mere mortal. Nations, cultures, arts, civilization — these are mortal, and their life is to ours as the life of a gnat. But it is immortals whom we joke with, work with, marry, snub, and exploit — immortal horrors or everlasting splendours. This does not mean that we are to be perpetually solemn. We must play. But our merriment must be of that kind (and it is, in fact, the merriest kind) which exists between people who have, from the outset, taken each other seriously — no flippancy, no superiority, no presumption. And our charity must be a real and costly love, with deep feeling for the sins in spite of which we love the sinner — no mere tolerance or indulgence which parodies love as flippancy parodies merriment. Next to the Blessed Sacrament itself, your neighbour is the holiest object presented to your senses."

C.S. Lewis, "The Weight of Glory"

Table of Contents

Introduction

This tale is a collection, a bouquet of delicate, complex subjects whose stories have been plucked and arranged in a vase by the kitchen window. Their variety of structure and color enlivens the room which before was merely a workspace, a means to a meal. It would certainly seem that He who adorns the flowers, who concocts the intricacies of flavor, and who fashions the souls of men finds beauty in them all.

Every human soul possesses intrinsic value simply because it has been formed in the image of God Himself. In her profound children's book *The Jesus Storybook Bible*, Sally Lloyd-Jones describes the pivotal moment God created mankind in this way: "And when God saw them he was like a new dad. 'You look like me,' he said…God loved them with all of his heart. And they were lovely because he loved them." In that perfection of Eden, humans were loved not for being special, nor for possessing any certain skill set, nor for being of any particular caliber, but simply for being.

Ideally, then, each person should perfectly reflect God's likeness as His image bearer. But in our own hearts and in the brokenness surrounding us, we can clearly see that all is not right. Sin entered the world when those first humans willfully disobeyed God's design, and as a result, each beautiful soul has become, as of yet, a broken, distorted replication of God's portrait. By His grace, various aspects of His character still shine through His defective vessels here on earth. His justice, kindness, faithfulness, and goodness are not foreign concepts. But as we long for the day when He will make all things right again, our fragmented hearts bend low to pick up the shards and piece back together that broken image of Eden.

To be human is to sense this loss, this disjunction. Heartbreak stalks us not only in the dark corners of funeral homes but also in each breath that whispers, "Life is not as it should be."

One of our unflattering human tendencies is to deal ourselves an abundance of grace, justifying our thoughts or behavior because we have access to all the details of our own circumstances. But lacking that intimate knowledge of others and their stories, we deal harshly with those who do not think or act like we do. However, the people in our spheres have not only travelled different roads than we have, they often drag along baggage we may never fully realize on their journeys we can never fully understand.

Each person has a backstory. And each of their tales is being released back into the world in the form of judgments or joys, bitterness or beauty. But because we cannot fully know another person, in their entire life's story or even in the immediate run-down of their day, we can never truly understand the depth of their feelings, why people live and joke and hide and explode like they do.

Some of the stories in the following pages are true, and some are truer than we would often like to admit. Too many fascinating, intricate people pass through our lives and yet remain misunderstood or merely missed. Although a work of fiction, this story details the people in your life. The people in your local pharmacy. They are the ones who are too loud in the dollar store or too quiet on the weekly conference call. They may even be you.

But after you have read these stories and peered into these hearts, you will do your own soul a great disservice if you look up from these pages and do not see all the complex, beautiful people in your world, the ones who are lovely simply because He loves them.

NEVER A MERE MORTAL

Written by

Devon Dial

1

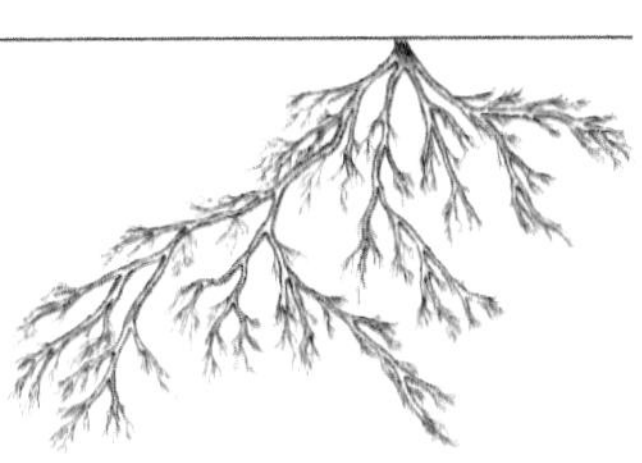

Stamps

If I can't be a river. Those are the words he had used, and though I agreed, they had picked at a loose thread on the fringe of my mind. This is a small town, one of those places through which people pass without pause. If they did stop, they might find something amazing here, some mesmerizing lunge at the soul that both swells like stringed music and haunts like the dark of a lonely road.

Instead, they judge our cramped homes and modest dreams. They drive past our old dilapidated barns and glance at our dogs eating grass beside the cars parked in the front yard. They look, but they never see the people who live in these homes and love these dogs and keep these cars in the yard because they belonged to our late fathers who never could quite get them running.

Although hopeful, his words had voiced a twinge of the homesickness that falls heavily on the far side of an ever-revolving heart. I know he has seen far more of the world than I have, but around here, we are all raindrops – small drips on the windshield that are quickly swished away.

As I had unloaded the items from his shopping basket, I slid a book of stamps across the scanner. Our conversation had started out like most of mine do when I'm wearing my green vest and name tag.

"Hello," I said. "You find everything okay today?"

"Yeah, sure did. Thanks," he replied, distractedly scanning the candy near the register before his gaze came to rest on some postcards by the door. "You from around here?"

When I nodded, he told me one of the postcards looked just like a place he used to vacation as a child, a little lake house nestled in the hills of Georgia.

It was a simple lake house, a little place on the point jutting out into the water where the river bends. Then TVA came in and decided to dam the river, so the little place on the bend was now sitting on a lengthy bit of recreational lakeshore, dwarfed by the multi-million-dollar vacation homes of celebrities.

In the wintertime when TVA drew down most of the water, the children used to walk the riverbed looking for arrowheads or toys they had dropped from the dock during the summer. They played "leap the lake" where it got so narrow they could bound right across to the other side. They built fires and roasted marshmallows and crammed too many people into that little lake house for Christmas. But the place never ran out of room – it just kept giving way and giving more.

"That red clay stained every pair of socks we had," he laughed, remembering the days that he pulled on his rubber boots and adventured with his brother and sisters through the mud along the water. The little ruffians always trusted the sludge to support their weight for one more step. It never did, and they never learned, and life was good.

And in the summers, they swam across and picked up rocks from the other side – proof they had made it across. Those boundary stones still line the front flower beds and serve as paperweights on the desk upstairs.

"You can't swim across now, with all the boats and crazy folks. You'd get run over. But man, that place back in the day…" And he had sighed with longing, yearning for the moment of time as much as the place itself. But places are the keepers of memory, the closest a person can get to recovering the good old days. He pines for the lake house but mostly for its ability to preserve the happy days of his childhood.

But now, that momentary snapshot doesn't exist any more. The lake house itself still stands, but that spot in his heart does not. Sure, if he looks out the squeaky screen door, he can still see the mountain sunsets down the lake. And lying in a hammock at the summer's end, he can still hear the breeze rustle through the treetops as autumn approaches.

"But it's not the same, either," he tried to explain. "Because generations of voices who narrated the family videos have passed on. And then you try to shoulder the camcorder, to take up the mantle, but your voice is just too weak to give the memories their proper weight. I went back to see it again a few weeks ago, and everything's the same and nothing is."

That stubborn red clay still stains every chance it gets. Those gentle waves still slap the dock as little feet squelch through muddy shallows, children reaching down to scoop up handfuls of mud for facials that are, perhaps, too organic. But now, even though it's his grandchildren who are flooding the boots and throwing the rocks and making the mud mustaches, his soul is the one that is just so tired.

He has experienced griefs that have wrenched his heart and threatened his faith, that have shaken the solid ground he took for granted. And running down the gravel path to the apple orchard and finding it overrun with weeds only served to remind him of the things he has lost.

"Or maybe the things I've found," he mused, "I'm not sure. Because I used to think that if I could just get to the place, I'd be back in that fortress of childhood innocence, where life waited for me while I took my time. And then to get there a few weeks back and find the apples rotting on the ground, and the old wood windows replaced, and the dirt road paved – it almost looks like progress, but it feels like pain. This isn't how things were, and yet here they are."

The red shore continues to erode, even as he gathers it with his memories and struggles to form it into the mud bowls he used to bake in the oven. Pounding, pressing, trying to make things be the way they were, stay the way they were…but unable to return to that place once again.

"It's like – who was that woman, the lonely lady from the eighteenth or nineteenth century who wrote all those poems?" he had asked vaguely.

The cashier shrugged and confessed she didn't like poetry. He laughed.

"Before my mom passed away, she recited one line of hers that's always stayed with me. Anyway it goes, 'That it will never come again is what makes life so sweet.' It seems to get truer as I get older. Oh, Dickinson. Emily Dickinson."

He said he regrets taking it all for granted back then. He wishes he had spent a few more nights playing his guitar down on the dock, listening to the voices across the lake drifting along the still water. He wishes he had spent a few more afternoons on that porch swing, just swinging. He wishes he had made more pies with his mom, actually enjoying the apples and not just pelting his brother with them.

"Maybe," he said, "I just wish I'd put that whole lake house and those days in a juicer and just pressed and squeezed and kept right on squeezing. That was the world back then, and I figured it'd always be like that – just 'keep on keeping on,' like my granddad always said."

She had nodded with a knowing smile. Her granddad used to say that, too. She picked up a pear to scan it, but it slipped from her grasp and bounced from the scanner to the floor. She apologized and offered to get him another.

"No, thanks though," he waved her aside, deep in his own thoughts. "I don't know, it was just a simpler time. I mean, we got dirty in that muddy water, but it all washed out at the end of the day. Or you just wore those clothes anyway."

"Yeah, I know what you mean," she said, letting the conversation lapse. He glanced back at the postcards and opened his mouth to speak but changed his mind. She punched a few buttons on the register and told him his total.

"I'll say this, then I'll let you get back to it – " he started again.

"No rush," she interrupted, checking her watch. "I've got another four and a half hours and not another customer in sight." *Plus*, she thought, *sometimes it's nice to meet another human.*

"Well, then I'll just say – I sometimes feel like life's just hurtling by at the speed of technology, and I'm afraid that I'll never be able to just stop and make something meaningful of my life, you know? Being back at that lake house, I started thinking that if I could choose, I'd want to be something like a river, carving my way into that muddy landscape. People wouldn't have any doubt that I'd been here, that I had changed my world in some way – you know, hopefully for the good."

"Yeah," the cashier said. She wasn't exactly sure where he was going, but she tried to follow along.

He glanced down before continuing, "But maybe God's check on the human ego is that He makes us raindrops instead of rivers." Although he looked straight into her eyes, his gaze ran past her and lodged much deeper into himself. She wondered if perhaps he had been a river as a younger man. "I mean, you admire the things because they're so impressive, but left unchecked, they destroy a lot of beautiful things as they rage through."

He pulled out his wallet and began to sift through his bills, as if to signal the end of his thoughts. As the cashier opened the drawer, he concluded – finally presenting what, she believed, he had been trying to put into words all along.

"And so I'm a raindrop," he said, and he turned to meet her eyes again, seeing her this time. "But if that's what I have to be, then I want to be a raindrop in the sand. I don't want to be another drop in the ocean, a drip in the bucket, just a quick splash into the puddle of what has already been. At least in the sand, I've moved something, changed something, maybe even left a little something of myself behind....You know, if I can't be a river."

And she does, she knows exactly what he means.

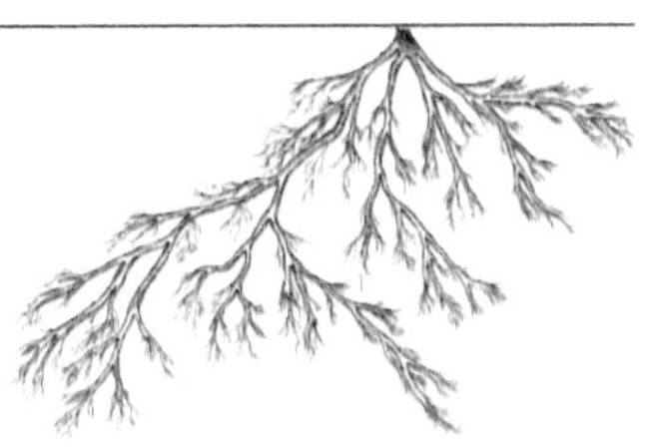

2

Copies and Faxes

Well, I hadn't planned on going there today. Poor cashier got an earful – bet they don't pay her enough for that. It was just supposed to be a quick stop for a snack and some stamps before I hit the road again.

"Bet you thought us old folks had things figured out a little better than that," I say with a chuckle. She is silent for a moment, as though she's unsure of how to answer the question without offending me.

"One thing I've learned," she offers, "well, people are putting that Tolkien quote on every journal, mug, and pillow they can find. I'm sure you've seen the one that says, 'Not all who wander are lost.' But anyway, one thing I've found, even here in a small town, is that the reverse can be just as true."

Not all who are lost are wandering. I'm still thinking over her words as I walk back outside into the beautiful autumn day, sliding out of the way of a stooped older woman who nearly runs into me. She's likely a couple of years younger than me, but life seems to have aged her disproportionately. *Maybe drugs.* She mumbles to herself as she clutches a tattered folder to her chest and walks past without a word to me – she is on a mission.

Every few days, Ms. Ruby collects her precious folder and

visits the supermarket. Each time she opens the door and marches over to the customer service desk, the employees busy themselves with tasks that gain a sudden urgency. Oblivious to their disregard, she steps up to the counter and announces that she needs to make copies and send some faxes on her account.

Her "account" is the special creation of the supermarket owner, a man who met Ms. Ruby a couple months ago and saw through her demands a familiar need to be human, to have a purpose. On that particular day, he was manning the service desk when she walked in, clutching that folder in both hands and mumbling to herself about the inefficiency of public transportation.

"Can I help you, ma'am?" he had asked.

She looked him over with a scowl, sizing him up with a condescending glance. He was found lacking. "I'd like to speak to the owner here."

"That'd be me," he said. "What can I do for you?"

"You? Hmm…Okay, I need to set up an account here. I walk almost everywhere and sometimes take the bus, so I don't carry cash for my safety. Other than my bus fare. But I send these faxes very often, so you'll be getting my regular business. These have to be sent today, so just put them on my account."

She had come to the right place. He would not risk much in the cost of her faxes if she failed to pay, and his pride deferred to his kindness.

"Alright then, ma'am," he said, pulling a notepad and pen out of the drawer. "What's your name?"

"Ruby."

"Alright, Ms. Ruby," he nodded, "it's good to meet you. This is how we'll keep up with your account." He wrote "Ms. Ruby's Account" across the top of the sheet in large letters. "We'll keep a running total of your purchases here on this piece of paper, and at the end of each day's dealings, we'll have you sign beside the new total on your account. Your signature is your word that you'll pay."

"Of course I'll pay. I have money," she stated sharply.

"Yes ma'am, I believe you."

"Okay," she said, opening her folder. "I need to send some important faxes to the White House. I don't have their fax number, so you'll need to call them to ask. I do have the phone number here."

He waited while she went through her large stack of papers.

"Here it is," she said, sliding the paper across the counter. "Just call and ask them for the fax number." So he did. "And write it down below for me, please, so I don't have to keep calling them for it." So he did.

"Okay, it's these fifteen pages here," she announced after sifting through the sheets for several minutes. It was fifteen pages consisting of typeset sections, handwritten notes, and newspaper clippings that had been taped together in a methodical but elementary fashion.

"Well these won't run through my machine, Ms. Ruby," he began. She frowned impatiently at him as he explained. "The machine will destroy these pages all cut and taped together like this. It'll only take single sheets that haven't been collaged together."

"Then make a copy of the pages and fax the copies," she said. So he did. That day, he spent three and a half hours with Ms. Ruby, making copies and sending fax after fax to the White House on her behalf.

She began coming in two or three days each week, opening that folder and requesting those copies. And faxing, always faxing.

As they assisted her, the employees sneaked glances at the faxes to determine what issue could warrant so many faxes to the President. Mostly, the pages talked about the national Department of Health and Human Services. Sometimes they were sheets of numbers – budgets, perhaps. Sometimes they were collaged essays of the history or the significance of the department crudely fashioned together using scissors and tape like the work of a first grader.

She was always mumbling while she compiled those documents. She often complained to herself about the employees' inabilities to make high-contrast copies or to feed the pages slowly through the machine, even as they stood before her.

For all those hours of work they put into sending those faxes, they never did find out if the White House received them. They never saw a response. All they knew is that when Ms. Ruby walked through the door, an unlucky employee was likely going to spend a minimum of two hours assisting her with those urgent federal correspondences.

But back before she marched into the store to send faxes, before she had "gone off the deep end," she was a financial genius. Over the years, she worked as an advisor who saved her clients' homes and ventures time and again. Her prowess in finance attracted attention and clients from across the nation.

Day after day, she worked diligently, rarely taking a sick day or vacation. She had grown up in the industry, watching her father as he worked tirelessly for those who entrusted their wealth to him. In this way, the world of finance was to her like an aloof uncle – sometimes agreeable, sometimes grumpy, but easy enough to get along with if you learned to read his mood.

When she was just eight years old, a bleary-eyed Ruby had stumbled into her father's office late one night to find him still at his work, poring over some papers with a pencil in hand. He noticed her shadow on the wall and glanced up at her.

"I had a bad dream," she said.

"I'm sorry to hear it, Rube. And what plagues the mind of the young princess?" he asked with a kind smile. "Troubles in your kingdom?"

"Some monsters were trying to get me," she said.

Her father frowned. "I'm sorry, baby. What happened? Did you shoot at them with your super-scary-staple-shooter?"

Ruby giggled and shook her head as he slid aside some papers on his desk to retrieve his stapler.

"You didn't? Well, that's the problem, princess. You always have to keep your staple-shooter handy."

Although she laughed, Ruby watched with great interest as he snapped the stapler open to create a sleek linear weapon.

"Watch this," he said. He clicked the stapler twice and two U-shaped pieces of metal flicked into the carpet. "You're armed now. No one can get you. Now off to bed."

Ruby excitedly took the stapler from him and ran back to her bedroom as her father stooped to pick up the staples and settled back to his work.

When she went in to wake up her daughter for school the next morning, Ruby's mother was horrified to find the stapler under Ruby's pillow. At Ruby's insistence that "Daddy gave it to me," her mother summoned him from the breakfast table, and they withdrew to the kitchen for several minutes of quiet debate. When they reemerged, Ruby's father called her to him.

"So you stayed safe last night, I see. No more villains after you?"

"No, I kept the stapler with me all night, but I never had to use it," Ruby said proudly.

"That's probably for the best, Rube. You know, with nightmares, the monsters are only in your mind and the darkness just amplifies how scary they feel – "

"But they seemed real," Ruby insisted.

"Absolutely," he agreed. "I have dreams like that, too. And they can feel so realistic that sometimes you just want to have a way to protect yourself – you know, a weapon in your hand."

"Yes, a super-scary-staple-shooter."

"Yes," he smiled, "though your mother has made a good point that it might actually be better to occasionally be frightened by pretend monsters than to take a friendly-fire staple to the face in the middle of the night. Maybe we'll use our imaginary staple-shooters in the future, just for safety."

Ruby had inherited the mind of her father, receiving all of its brilliance and, in time, all of its brokenness. As a child, she had wanted to grow up to be just like him. His creativity inspired her own imagination. Cardboard boxes evolved into barns, palaces, and cathedrals in his hands. It was as if every story came to life as he spoke, every financial forecast arrived as he had predicted...until the year when his genius seeped over that thinning line and the monsters in his mind overstepped their nighttime bounds.

It went quickly, his mind. At first, twenty-year-old Ruby saw very few signs that things were amiss – a forgotten name here, a missed event there. Then his mind began to attack all he had known until he could no longer discern the horrors haunting his mind from the clients supporting his business.

"He's lost it," they said, "gone crazy." But what they could not realize while they lobbed their statements from a safe distance away is that his mind was only the first thing to go. Following in quick succession, he also lost his work, his reputation, and his daughter's respect.

Initially, Ruby bore the embarrassment admirably, continuing to discuss his odd opinions and to introduce him to her friends when he came to the university. But his loud conspiracy theories became harder to excuse, his outbursts harder to hide. Outwardly, he still looked like her father, the one who had created her world, but now he voiced strange ideas she could not follow – he was no longer the man she had always admired.

After much debate, she finally convinced her mother to place him in a home. He needed to get help for his unstable mind, which constantly threatened to whisk him away. She selected a place only two hours from her school, where she would be able to check in on him frequently.

Back at the university, Ruby threw herself into her studies as she tried to avoid the sad places in her mind. She set out to make a name for herself, to prove that she could achieve more than the future for which she feared she, too, was destined.

It was in the midst of this striving that she met Paul, who was all that her father had been and then ceased to be. After their first conversation, she loved him for the nostalgic way he felt like home. They saw each other for only six months before Paul asked her father to give him permission to marry Ruby, despite her insistence that the tradition was unnecessary. As she had feared, her father questioned Paul's intentions and interrogated him about his family and their ties to secret societies. Paul looked him in the eye and answered with the sincerity owed a respectable man raising relevant concerns. Ultimately, when her father received satisfactory answers to his questions, he relented and gave his approval in the form of a dramatic blessing, which he pronounced over them while standing in his chair with his arms extended.

That had been only two months before her father's physical health began slipping through his fingers, following his mind quickly over the cliff just as the chains on a prisoner's ankles slide swiftly after the iron ball. When he passed on a Wednesday, Ruby cried for the man she had lost so long ago, grieved the cruelty of a world that would take her father before it took his body, leaving her to untangle her grief and her guilt. They buried him two days later at a private ceremony. Ruby spent the weekend looking through old pictures, then woke Monday morning resenting the relief she felt, the sense that his absence would make her future shine a little more brightly.

Only a few years later, she and her husband welcomed a baby boy, Charlie. And every morning, they sang a lively rendition of an old song to him –

> *Greet the world, Charlie,*
> *The sun shines for you,*
> *Love the world, my boy,*
> *And it'll adore you.*

It was a song loosely based on one that Ruby's father used to sing to her when she was a little girl, but Paul thundered it each morning with operatic vibrato to Charlie's delight. The boy beamed as they celebrated his waking each day, and when he could talk, he joined in serenading himself every morning.

But the sun would not always shine for Charlie nor for Ruby. They had sung their song and eaten their breakfast as usual on the morning their lives changed forever. After she dropped Charlie off at school, Ruby got the call. Paul was gone, found unresponsive in his office. Ruby later learned that an undetected heart issue had led to a massive heart attack.

Ruby's mind stiffened. Paul had been a steadying force whenever she expressed fears that her mind would eventually unravel as her father's had. Paul's was the calm voice of reassurance, reminding her of his promise "for better or for worse – whatever we walk through, we'll do it together." He had quieted her doubts about her future, her worries for Charlie's world.

Although Ruby had worked tirelessly to provide for Charlie, it was Paul who had patiently taken a knee to show his son the beauty of the world around him.

"It's like this, Charlie, just a little bit rounded here like a whale belly and then a straight line," Paul had instructed his young son one evening as he guided the boy's hand to outline a leaf on the driveway. He'd arrived home from work to find Charlie drawing with chalk on the driveway while Ruby prepared their dinner. They glanced up to see Ruby watching them from the open kitchen window.

"Oh no, my boy," Paul exclaimed loud enough for her to hear. "It looks like your mom has been captured by the Work Monster. We need to rescue her!"

Paul grabbed an empty paper towel tube from the garage and handed it to his son as they rushed into the house. Paul took Ruby into his arms as he snatched her from her work, and Charlie – zealous in his misunderstanding of the task at hand – smacked her on the leg with his pretend sword. Ruby laughed, just as she would laugh nearly every day when Paul arrived home after work. Like her father, Paul brightened her world and dispelled her fears, pushing the monsters back into the shadows.

After Paul's death, Ruby knew that she could and would go on, that one day she would be okay again. She had to be, if only for little Charlie. But she never could bring herself to sing the song to him again. That song had been hers, but the laughter had been Paul's. When he was torn away from them, the laughter was wrenched away first and the song followed soon after.

The melody fading, Ruby immersed herself in her work, clawing for success to dull the pain of Paul's absence and to bring meaning to her existence. After many years, she had earned her reputation as a talented, if relentless, financial expert.

Ruby never again found a love like Paul's. Once, many years later, she had invited a colleague home for dinner after a few engaging lunch conversations. Sitting at the table in Paul's vacant seat, he had asked Charlie some questions about his school during dinner, and Ruby had smiled to see Charlie's face brighten at his attention.

When Charlie brought out his rock collection after dinner, their guest humored him for several minutes as they admired the smooth stones. But when Charlie ran off to his room to find his fool's gold, Ruby's guest turned to her.

"Charlie's a great kid," he said as he laughed. "What time does he go to bed? I get tired just watching him play. All that energy, wasted on the young, right?"

She smiled and nodded, slowly comprehending her colleague's hint. She had tucked Charlie into bed early that night, her lonely heart uneasily sandwiched between its own longings and the unsteady sense that Charlie could tumble from his place.

"No one can love this boy like we did, Paul," she had cried into her pillow that night. And, in her mind, that was that, and she sealed that section of her heart, refusing to entertain the idea ever again.

She threw herself into her work and eventually was thrown back out of it as her father's illness trickled down into her mind. Uncomfortable with the way stillness opened the door into a bottomless deep, Ruby factored at all hours of the day and figured during every wakeful moment in the night. For years on end, she ran her clients' books in her mind continuously, always advancing, always grasping.

"Mom?"

"What is it, Charlie?" she asked her thirty-four-year-old son.

"You're doing it again…"

"Oh," Ruby smiled as she covered her face with her hands, "I'm sorry, son. It's just this message from my client – he wants to do things a certain way, a ridiculous way. He's paying me to know better but fights me when I say so. I guess I'm just going through the reasons with him in my – "

"You were talking to Dad. About me. Again."

"What?"

"You have to talk some sense into him, Paul," Charlie pleaded, doing his best impression of her voice. "The music is beautiful, but it isn't a stable job. Don't you think you could talk to him?"

"No, you must've misheard me. Your father isn't even here."

"I know that," Charlie countered bitterly. "We need to get you in to talk with someone."

These were conversations she was having far too regularly – first, the running conversation throughout the day with Paul and then this conversation at the kitchen table with Charlie. At first, Ruby fought the tendency to slide into that realm where Paul still remained by her side, wrestling to hold tight to reality. But as the years dragged on, the struggle exhausted her mind, and she began to slip.

Initially, Charlie called her back to reality, back to him, each time. But as her mind continued to drift, Ruby became aggressive in her defenses, clinging to fragments of reality and supplementing delusion in the gaps.

Charlie dropped by one afternoon and found her barricaded in her room. Pleading through the door, he finally persuaded her to come out to the kitchen to have a cup of tea with him. She sat down nearly touching his elbow and leaned in close.

"They could be listening to us right now, Charlie," she whispered, "Keep your voice down." She glanced furtively around the room, motioning to the air vents and windows.

"Who's *they?*" Charlie asked. She quickly placed a hand on his arm to quiet him.

"The ones who stole my garbage can. Last week it was my mail, and now it's my garbage can."

"Mom, trust me, no one wants to take your garbage. Plus, your can's still right there, around the side like always."

"No, that's not mine. They've swapped them out, thinking I wouldn't notice while they try to steal my information. But," she mouthed to him, "I don't put sensitive information in there."

Charlie laid his forehead on the table and closed his eyes. Her ideas were woven together with too many shoddy materials. It would take all day to follow just one thread of the mess to its logical end. *She's not choosing to be like this*, Charlie reminded himself. *Walk toward her.* And for years, he had. He made frequent excuses to visit and always took inventory of her fridge, dropping by later with a bag of groceries "because he was in the neighborhood."

But in the end, when her mind slapped away his offer to hold her feet to the ground, Charlie let her fly, a decision he would question every day of his life. She had been talking to Paul one evening about Charlie's musical aspirations when he walked out.

He said, "Mom, I'm Charlie," kissed her head, opened the front door, and stepped out.

He was never sure if he would have handled things differently if he had it to do over again, especially with "the Incident" that was to come years later. It would not be until he himself was old and gray that he realized he had always called it "The Incident" and not "The Accident," as if in his heart he feared she could have intentionally taken that step. *No, surely not*, he always reassured himself quickly, *she would never have done that*. And yet, he never did refer to "the Incident" in any other way.

Ruby could not understand the full implications of Charlie's leaving at the time, but she keenly felt his absence and missed his regular visits. So she fixated on what had caused the crumbling of her world: the inadequate systems for monitoring health which had failed her dear Paul.

If the doctors had evaluated him more frequently, they would have found the issue with his heart. If they had found it, they could have fixed it before it struck. If they had fixed it, he would still be here. If he was still here, her mind would have stayed sharp. And if her mind had stayed, Charlie would have, too. If she could only convince the Department of Health and Human Services to fix the broken systems, then maybe other women would be able to keep their husbands, minds, and sons.

Every couple of days, Ms. Ruby shuffles into the supermarket, talking to an invisible companion, recounting her day and reiterating the importance of her work. She sends urgent messages to the President, and the supermarket employees laugh because they are sure he does not see them. And if he does, they are sure he does not read them. And if he does, they are sure he laughs along at the absurdity.

"No, no no no," she says to the woman behind the counter. "You got it all out of order. Give me that back. I'll fix it, and then you can send it." She takes the stack of papers, muttering about the quality of minimum wage assistance. As she organizes the pages and hands them back to the woman, a disheveled man limps toward the door with a dirty backpack weighed down by all of his possessions.

"Pick up your hat," Ms. Ruby fusses at the man. "Phil, get your hat. It fell on the floor."

"Thanks, Ms. Ruby," he says with a sympathetic smile as he stoops to pick up the worn cap. Ms. Ruby drifts toward the checkout lines by the door, where a pretty young woman holds a children's puzzle in both hands. She glances curiously at Ms. Ruby.

"Oh I'm not cutting in line, just waiting on my fax to go through," Ms. Ruby offers as she looks over the woman and her simple puzzle. She frowns with confusion at the purchase.

"You ought to work on some more intricate puzzles, dear. At your age, I could do a 5000-piece puzzle by myself easily. Landscapes, animals, all kinds of puzzles. With lots of pieces."

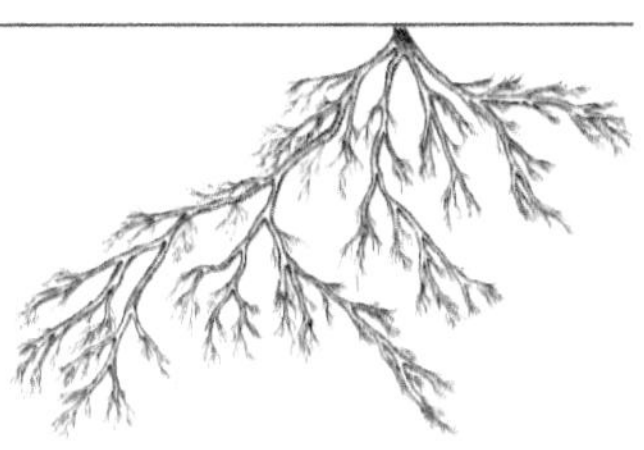

3

A Twelve-Piece Puzzle

"My son, even – he was doing 100-piece puzzles by the time he was eight," I say proudly. Charlie was actually doing 250-piece puzzles by then, but I don't want to embarrass her. "And puzzles keep the mind sharp so it's good to challenge yourself with some of the harder ones." *A real shame,* I think to myself. *I would be embarrassed to purchase a puzzle like that at her age.* She looks to the cashier, then responds to my encouragement with a confused smile and nod. *Poor dear, perhaps that puzzle really is the best she can do.*

But behind the upward turn of her mouth, the woman's heart twists as yet another person weighs in with advice for her day, insight for her life.

Back before she shopped for puzzles with only twelve pieces, she had had other dreams, none of which anticipated this life. Even as a young child, her parents had raised her to believe that with hard work and a little luck, she could be whatever she wanted to be.

"The clouds themselves will become the cobblestones under your feet," they had told her. "Just follow your heart as you pursue your dreams." And indeed, her early experiences confirmed that she need look no further than herself for success in each new venture. Fueled by this reassurance, she had no shortage of friends as she gave freely of herself and held nothing back for fear of rejection. Society smiled on her, and she met its gaze and smiled right back. In every undertaking, she confidently stepped forward and was validated by firm ground beneath.

"You are so lucky," her ninth-grade best friend said quietly, inspecting a new note from her latest secret admirer. "You don't even have to try – you just get good grades and all the guys' attention. It's not fair."

She had resented Jenny's charge.

"That's not true. I want good grades, so I make the time to study. I want to talk to boys, so I make myself start a conversation. You can't just sit back and complain, Jenny – things won't fall right into your lap."

"But," Jenny argued, "you don't even know it's possible to try something and fail. That's all I mean by 'lucky' – if you even attempt something, you succeed at it. Maybe someday you'll get what I mean."

But she did not for many years, as all things continued to fall predictably into line. The time she spent in the gym yielded the results she anticipated. Her sense of fashion, unhindered by insecurity, propelled her to the front of each trend as her outfits were approved and admired. Her intellectual pursuits were rewarded with degrees and new academic circles. The clouds themselves really did become the cobblestones beneath her steps, as each door she approached would open to reveal a more excellent path awaiting.

As expected, her peers in college were naturally drawn to her company, and she never lacked friendship or attention. Girlfriends flocked to her side, caught up in her spontaneous ideas and fun adventures. Men, too, basked in her presence as she boldly voiced her opinions without a hint of self-doubt. She dated many of them at different turns before repurposing the relationships with such tact that each rejected boyfriend considered himself to be a more special friend than the next.

But one young man surpassed the rest. He was nearly a male

reflection of herself in his charm and confidence. After dating for a year, both were fully convinced of their compatibility in almost every aspect. Their futures aligned, their personalities meshed, and their laughter could stitch the uneven places along the seams.

"Why not?" he had asked before their graduation, pulling a ring from his pocket as he dropped to one knee on a cool spring evening.

"If that's a proposal," she advised, "you ought to do it again." His face turned red, and they both laughed.

But then he did do it again, and much improved, so she agreed.

The first years of their marriage were relatively happy, though not always easy. Like many newlyweds, they had to learn the art of living not only for each other but with one another. The refining clashes were fierce but brief. As each selfish tendency appeared, it was named by the one, rationalized by the possessor, attacked and defended by turns, and eventually uprooted as they pulled together to preserve their relationship.

On the morning of their fourth anniversary, she got up early and hurried to the kitchen to make coffee as she always did. She fixed it like she always had and walked back to their bedroom. She sat down on the bed, running her fingers through her hair before gently patting his arm. When he opened his eyes and sat up in bed, she handed him the mug and watched his face expectantly. He took a sip and smiled at her.

"Well, good morning to you," he said sleepily. "What is it?"

"Do you notice anything different?" she asked. A dangerous question, especially first thing in the morning. He had not noticed anything different. Determined to avoid a conflict, he quickly studied her appearance.

"I really like your hair," he began, "and your body, and this coffee. And our sheets, and how clean our room is. And the shade of green on the bathroom walls really was the perfect choice – "

She laughed with him. "No, your mug," she hinted to narrow the field.

She had carefully handed it to him with the letters "D-A-D" facing him, but he had not noticed. As he saw it, his hands began to tremble.

"Are you? Are we…?" He put down the mug and threw off the covers as he took her in his arms. "We are? How long? When?" Thrilled that his excitement matched her own, she did her best to answer all of his half-formed questions, bursting with the details she no longer had to hide. They spent the next hour mapping out their pregnancy and their new life beyond.

The months of anticipation passed quickly as they vigorously kneaded their little home, stretching its short but welcoming arms to receive their newest addition. They converted the large walk-in closet to a small nursery and angled the kitchen table to allow more room for play.

"Do you want a boy or girl?" he asked one morning while he assembled a small bookshelf.

"I'm not really sure. I just want it to be healthy, you know? A little boy would be adorable, and you'd be so great with him," she said. "Plus, I hear little boys get really attached to their moms."

She considered the alternative. "But on the other hand, I could really enjoy a girl – all those tiny girly things, all the pink bows and lacy socks and little frilly dresses. There's just something enchanting about sharing my life with a little girl." She began speaking faster as she made a list. "Girls nights, fingernail polish, tutus and lace, ballet, little chats about school or boys or – "

"Well, I see you're pretty neutral," he cut in with a laugh, "so it'll be good you're so unbiased when we find out in a month."

But as it always had, the Hand that holds the universe opened to reveal yet another gift at their appointment. A girl. Seeing the profile of her little face, he whispered, "Bella. Gift of God's favor." She never had another name.

"A girl!" Their families rejoiced to hear a little princess would be joining the rowdy band of boy cousins. Their friends celebrated her upcoming arrival with extravagant gifts. A soft wave of pink rolled over Bella's nursery. Rosy plush elephants, fluffy coral pillows, little pink bath towels. Since the expression of their love was limited for the time being to the things they could purchase, the nursery brimmed with an overwhelming stockpile of "necessities."

One morning, her water broke as she walked to the mailbox. Fear and excitement gripped her as she hurried back inside to tell him the news. Within two hours, they were sitting in a hospital room, holding hands and as ready as they could ever be. She labored for the rest of the day and all through the night.

Bella arrived the following morning, and her mom and dad broke down with the raw emotion of fresh parenthood. They did not notice the subtle twitch of the doctor's brow, so they were not concerned when he casually mentioned that the nurses would have to take Bella from the room to run a couple of tests. He reassured them that she would be in good hands while Mom and Dad rested and regained their strength.

But they could never regain enough strength to prepare them for the diagnosis, for the shriveling of their dreams into the dark knot of grief they could not untangle.

"Now, Bella will likely still lead a very full and happy life, but as her parents, you will have to alter your expectations," the doctor began. "At this point, we don't know …" Bella's parents could no longer hear the words he said over the splintering of their dreams. They listened in misery as he spoke but would not fully comprehend his words until much later.

"A lot of that will be determined by your effort in working with her… It may take her a little longer than other children to reach those milestones, but she can, and with today's medical advances and therapies, she likely will…To be very honest with you, though, it will be a struggle…Especially these first few months, you'll have to work hard to support each other…"

It was an exhausting climb.

"A hard road ahead," the doctor had said. But that implied it was one that could and would be walked simply by placing one foot in front of the other. It did not account for the times they had to pull themselves along a ledge with arms that could not bear the weight of the moment. The late night scares, the surgeries, the therapies, the uncertain future, the frazzled arguments and unravelling dreams…on this new battlefield, they struggled to fight together against the enemy that clung to their precious daughter.

"I'll sit up with her tonight," Bella's father had insisted late one night after a particularly rough week.

"No, that's okay. I probably won't sleep anyway. You go ahead and rest."

"Babe, you've been at her side the past four nights. We've got the monitor in her room, and I'll be right here if she makes even the tiniest noise. You've got to get some sleep."

"I've got to help my daughter," she raised her voice in protest. "You heard the doctor, it all depends on how well we fight this for her. We can't sit idly by – "

"Well us not sleeping is definitely not going to help her, or us either," he said, his voice rising. "You're not doing any good just staying awake. All you're doing is running yourself into the ground. And that doesn't help anybody."

She burst into tears, angry at his blunt words that made sense but did not comfort her breaking heart. She was frustrated with how they now wasted so many conversations this way, with simple comments quickly escalating into quarrels. Even thoughtful suggestions sent them spiraling into uncharted territories where they mistrusted themselves and each other. They still deeply cared for each other, but now, they often fought as each tried to help their cherished baby girl.

It was lonely and not only within the walls of their home. Even her best friend Anna, who was familiar with a mother's grief, struggled to know how to be present in their pain. Their other friends, the bearers of the pink tide in Bella's nursery, did not understand the diagnosis or know what to say. So they said nothing.

Though they loved the grieving couple, their friends were desperately afraid to say the wrong thing, afraid to bring their happy news into a home needing temporary protection from the bright world. So they stayed away. And they hated themselves for saying nothing, but as time continued to drop from the hourglass grain by grain, it became more awkward to re-enter their wounded world. So they did not.

Furthermore, meeting new friends brought anguish for the outgoing couple who had never before struggled to make connections. They had never known what it was to extend themselves in friendship while balancing a fear that they might not be held securely on the other end.

When new neighbors moved in next door, Bella's dad caught them in their driveway as he arrived home that evening and introduced himself. He immediately befriended the amicable father of four, and the two men were still deep in conversation when Bella's mom came outside in search of her husband, whom she had expected for dinner a half hour ago. After a quick introduction, her husband invited the neighbors to come for dinner the following evening.

"Sounds great, good excuse to take a break from all of these boxes," the other father laughed. "What time?"

"How does six o'clock sound?"

"Great. Okay if we bring the kids?"

"Maybe just pick your favorite two or three," Bella's father said with a straight face before breaking into a laugh, and the neighbors joined him. "No! Bring them all! Our little girl Bella will love to meet you all."

When the family arrived the next evening, Bella was sorting her dolls by their friendliness so that she would be able to properly introduce each one to her new neighbors. The doorbell rang just as Bella was finishing her arrangements, and she ran into the living room to greet them.

"And this is Bella," her father announced as she ran over to hug the youngest child. Her father made a great show of trying to remember the new friends' names as he pointed to each down the line.

"Bella, this is Mr. Bill, Mrs. Layla, then Doug – no Dave?" he announced with a question. The boy laughed and nodded, so he continued down the line, naming and renaming the other children.

And with each introduction, as the neighbors greeted Bella, their faces would flicker with a quick, assessing glance before they could hide them again behind their smiles.

Every single time. Although Bella's parents had come to know and even expect this reaction over the years, these introductions scratched at their happiness each time, defacing their earnest wish that the world would one day see Bella clearly.

Her parents pretended not to notice the assessments as their daughter's appearance was silently appraised and classified with a label, but each quick analysis was a dagger to her mother's heart. Bella's genuine smile, her pleasure in the ordinary treasures of this beautiful life – all stripped of their purity and pressed into a mold that could be more neatly known and understood.

And Bella's parents knew the importance of their daughter being understood. Other children regularly shied away from Bella, fearing her appearance as if she were scary, her presence as if she were contagious. Bella's mom always made a conscious effort to explain, to help her daughter find acceptance, but she often feared for Bella's future.

While she was out shopping with her girl, she noticed when other shoppers avoided eye contact with them. Or worse, when they had entire conversations with her over Bella's head.

"Oh my, she's adorable," one woman had remarked last week as they shopped for cat food. "Does she have a kitten at home?"

Just ask her. She loves to talk about Mittens, her heart wept. *Ask Bella, she'd love to tell you.*

But whoever had created this isolated existence forgot to inform Bella of its hardship. She greeted each morning with great expectations, which were fulfilled daily before bedtime. Every flower was a gift, every bug a fascinating study. Every person was a genuine friend.

Bella, eager observer that she was, was perhaps more importantly a teacher in her zest for life. And Bella's mom, who had spent the better part of her life drowning in pools of conventional beauty and conditional love, came to see the essences of true beauty and pure love in the spirit of her daughter.

Just earlier this week, they had stumbled upon one of those

unlooked-for happy days. Bella's mom had learned to treasure these as gifts from the great Giver, especially when she compared them to her own meticulously planned outings – when she had scheduled around nap times, packed snacks, coordinated outfits, and brought her camera to capture the fun. But the naps never happened when they were supposed to, the snacks were the wrong ones, the outfits were stained before the picturesque moments. These occasions most often ended in frustration and meltdowns from either Bella or her mom, often both.

But this had been one of those moments that sprang upon them through no planning of their own. As they drove home from a friend's house, Bella spotted a little pond and asked if they could stop to see what fish lived in it. Her mom, who had no other plans for the afternoon, stopped the car, and they walked to the water's edge hand-in-hand. But Bella stepped too close to the water, and her shoe plunged through the deceptive grass straight into the pond as Bella stumbled backward and sat heavily on the bank. Her mom had nervously watched her reaction – Bella loved these shoes and did not love wet feet.

But that day, she laughed. A hearty, bubbling release of joy as she laid back on the grass and cackled. Her mom joined, and they spent several minutes lying there before Bella pulled herself up and began picking flowers.

"Look!" she exclaimed suddenly, pointing into the water. Sitting up, Bella's mom leaned over to see minnows darting along the edge of the pond. She smiled to herself. A beautiful afternoon with water and flowers and tiny fish. *One of those unlooked-for happy days.*

"Love you," Bella said, offering her mom the handful of weeds. Her mom smiled back.

"Love you, girlie. Oh, thank you," she said, taking the bouquet. "Let's put these in water when we get home. They're beautiful."

Then looking back out over the water, she closed her eyes and breathed the words again.

Thank you. In spite of the uncertain future, Bella's mom had begun to realize that she did not need to have full control of her life to appreciate the joys which had been carefully sprinkled along the way for her indulgence.

Time had gently shifted her dreams to more peacefully align with her reality, but Bella had done much more: she had given her parents new depths that made their days brighter than they had been when their dreams had been one-dimensional.

Bella's mom had learned to reshelve the feelings that fell each time people offered their thoughts, condolences, and grim nods, her emotions clattering to the hard ground beneath her feet, which had turned out to be cobblestones, solid rock yet nothing more.

But today, though the woman's words about the puzzle sting, Bella's mom smiles and nothing falls. She glances at the thin girl behind her in line, the one hugging a shrink-wrapped DVD to her chest. Hearing the older woman's comments, the slight woman shakes her head and rolls her eyes irritably in the woman's direction. Bella's mom smiles back graciously. After all, today is a good day. She is heading home with a surprise: a puzzle for the most beautiful girl in the world.

4

Season Three

Back before the arrival of my beautiful girl, when people steadily looked me in the eye, I used to get caught up watching all the latest television programs, too. I remember spending hours figuring out the mysteries and solving the murders, but it's been years since I've allowed myself to do that. I pretend I'm looking past her, this skinnier thirty-year-old version of who I might've become, but I let my eyes hover for a few seconds over the spine, straining to see the series title. I try to figure out what tonight's entertainment will be in another home where worries are checked at the door and life's biggest concern is how many episodes I can watch tonight and still wake up for work in the morning.

As I let my eyes linger too long, the woman turns to look back at me. She smiles kindly, and I shrug to brush off the older woman's comments, but I can follow only a part of what her smile conveys.

Jessica has not always gone home to an empty house, tossing her bag into the empty chair and switching on the television to fill the empty room with the white noise of canned laughter. She has not always withdrawn to her couch every evening, watching hours of dramas she does not care about, staying up too late with characters who care nothing for her, just to avoid the thoughts that crouch in the shadows.

Back then, before the Dark fell like a cloak over her world, she had spent every spare minute pursuing her hobbies. There were so many that she often felt like an old cat lady who had to set aside time for each so that none would feel neglected. She had managed to keep up with her elementary school girlfriends for years. She still smiled to see the old photos showing all the fun and awkward phases of their friendship. *Looking at you, braces.*

In high school, the girls began going on adventures together. All four of them loved the outdoors, and they frequently camped together. Jessica loved sleeping under the boundless sky without feeling the weight of its vastness, distributed as it was over their community of four.

The group had fizzled during their junior year of high school, when two of the girls moved away and Amanda started dating a weirdo. *Zack Zustan, I wonder where he is now.* Back then, he called himself Dr. Zeus and had an annoying habit of giving all of his classmates mythological nicknames based on their personalities, which was amusing for only his strange little group of friends. Naturally, Jessica began to spend less time with Amanda where Dr. Zeus was involved until the girls rarely spoke.

Although she missed her friends, Jessica was not unhappy to find herself with more time alone. Even after she started dating, Jessica discovered an inclination toward solitude she had not known her heart to need, and she hiked the trails and soothed her soul in the quiet of the woods. In those days, she had kept company with the poets and listened to the heart songs that so beautifully expressed her feelings. She kept journals of her own poems and short stories based on her experiences in the woods.

One Saturday morning, she had visited the library in search of a book to take on the trail. She had arranged a purposefully empty day, so she chose an obscure book of poetry and drove to her beloved pocket of wilderness about an hour and a half outside of town.

She hiked for a while before she came to the river, swollen with the recent rain. The large, flat rocks beckoned, so she settled herself on her stomach on a stone that looked like a turtle.

"Let's see what you have to say, Mr. Arnold," she said aloud, reading the name on the title page. "Mr. Matthew Arnold of the 1800s." She opened the book randomly to a poem called "The Buried Life." The peaceful scenery and antiquated language nearly lulled her to sleep, and she read each line several times, struggling to concentrate:

> *Light flows our war of mocking words, and yet,*
> *Behold, with tears mine eyes are wet!*
> *I feel a nameless sadness o'er me roll.*
> *Yes, yes, we know that we can jest,*
> *We know, we know that we can smile!*
> *But there's a something in this breast —*

Jessica sat up as she continued to read. "To which thy light words bring no rest…" She labored through the rest of the poem, sensing a great discovery immediately, though it would take several readings before she could fully grasp its meaning. Reading the words again, she caught her breath. *Why is no one talking about this? Some guy in the 1800s writes a poem and here I sit feeling like maybe for the first time, someone understands. Somebody gets it.*

She had gone home inspired to write meaningful verses like that. For the next year, she had enjoyed the freedom and accomplishment she felt as she gave voice to her heart's deepest longings.

But then her words had evaporated. It was as if a dark tide had dragged her talent away, snatching her expression like lapping waves eroding the shoreline of a recreational lake. The retreat of her personality into itself had occurred so gradually that she had not even noticed the waning of her world. When she stopped to take deliberate inventory, she could sense the shift in herself as she lost interest in her hobbies, avoided the friends who had enjoyed them with her, and craved the empty space of sleep.

These days, she did not have much to write because she was unable to pierce through the Dark. When she could not muster the energy for her interests any more, could not spark the desire for the things that had always made her feel most alive, she found herself apologizing to a better version of herself from days long gone.

Many nights, she drifted into a recurring dream in which she was holding a gray balloon by a string as she walked along the sidewalk in a fancy neighborhood. An eerie sunset spread shockingly cold hues of blue and green across the sky. As she walked, she would gradually become aware of a child with a teddy bear following behind at a distance.

Although he was only about four years old, he would inevitably gain ground until he stood right in front of her, speaking enthusiastically while blocking her way. Slightly unnerved by the unattended child, she would look for his mother but was never able to find her. She attempted to answer the child's unending chatter, but in her dream she was frozen, unable to reply. This, however, did not seem to discourage the child, and he would continue babbling unfazed, becoming more and more excited as he spoke.

On waking, she could never recall what he had said. All she could remember is that as he talked, she understood less and less of the child's speech, his voice becoming more distorted as he became more animated. As the dream progressed, his words tumbled out at an alarming rate as he waved his hands frantically back and forth between her and the balloon until Jessica realized that he wanted to have a closer look at it.

Casting another hopeful glance around for his mother, Jessica would grab the balloon between her hands and hold it low for him to see. And each time, he would press the teddy bear's nose into the balloon as though to pop it, but its blunt nose could never quite break through. Instead, he pushed the bear into the balloon until it was face to face with her, with its fearful eyes staring wildly into hers as though it was suffocating in that gray world from which it could not escape. Then Jessica would wake up with a shiver and will herself to get out of bed. Some days she was successful, and some days she was not.

Although she was no stranger to feelings like these, this was a new and different kind of darkness. Back in college, she had experienced the common angst that came with charting out her course, hammering out her dreams. She had known what it was to feel isolated and overwhelmed at the same time, had driven down many a lonely back road during a thunderstorm just to see the drops spatter her windshield even as unexplained tears speckled her lap.

But back in those days, the dilemmas were usually short-lived and treatable with excursions into nature. There had been some dark days, but they had had edges she could see even in the night – edges that hinted these times were temporary, that promised these shadows were fleeting.

This was not that. This pulled her deeper into itself by pulling her further into herself like a black hole. As hard as she clawed to escape, the Dark was always there, always pulling. She could not draw back the curtain because she could not find the edges; she could not fight the demons because they had no shape. Some days, it was too much to get out of bed, and sleep provided the only escape.

"You missed the monthly birthday celebration at work yesterday," Cathy had said, dropping by her office one morning with a piece of cake on a paper plate. "Don't worry – I saved you a piece. It's red velvet, and it was going fast." People joked that Cathy was the "work mother" around the office. She always checked in to see that her coworkers were well, or at least well-fed.

"I figured you must've been sick. Or maybe just partied too hard on your own?" She winked.

"Definitely something like that," Jessica laughed. "No, honestly, I didn't feel too good."

"Oh really? More like allergies or like a stomach bug?" Cathy pressed, setting the plate on her desk. "I've heard of several people with sinus stuff. I think we're hitting that time of year where the crud starts making its rounds."

"Oh, I think it was probably just something I ate," Jessica lied. When she had opened her eyes, she realized it was her birthday, took a couple of sleeping pills, and went back to bed. That had been her birthday, a hiding from the darkness that came with the morning.

She faced her birthdays now with a growing dread each year. When she was a child, they arrived with a sense of magic, a promise of great things yet unexperienced. Her parents planned elaborate parties she and her friends reminisced about all year long. As a younger woman even, she had looked forward to the celebrations with great anticipation. But now, like the pounding waves that stole far more than they brought, these milestones offered nothing but a glaring reminder of the ebbing away of her life.

How could I tell Cathy that there is nothing actually wrong, but that on the other hand, everything is upside down and I can't figure out how to flip it back? Jessica asked herself. *She'll think I'm crazy, like I sometimes do myself.*

"Oh okay," Cathy had said. "Well I'm glad you're feeling better… you are, right?"

"Yes, much better, thanks," Jessica lied again.

Unable to push back the Dark, she instead pushed back the friends who came too close, who asked the questions she wished she could answer. She made up excuses to avoid the questions and, in so doing, dodged the people who probed because they cared. She had even pushed away the man who had asked to walk at her side. He had tried to stay, but she had shut him out.

A musician who had struggled against shades of the Dark himself, he had willingly taken her hand to fight it beside her. He had helped her to keep it at bay by speaking truth in the face of the shapelessness that threatened to pull her under. He had been her best friend and her strongest support. In the end, she had released him, not because she did not love or desperately need him, but because she felt ashamed for condemning him to carry her burden into the bleak future.

She had been harsh in sending him away, fearing that anything less than a hard break would keep his hope alive. The day she pulled his parachute, releasing him from her burdens, was the loneliest of her life as she sent away the only hope of rescue on her horizon.

Each night, as she reached to turn off her lamp, her weary gaze settled on an early photo of them taken the day they had gone back to the library to return the old book of poems.

"Be free and fly, my love," she would whisper. "I'll be fine." She reassured herself that her tears were no indication to the contrary. She followed his success, tracing his late-night path on the posters she saw around town. She cheered for him from the shadows but was careful to follow from a leper's distance, always staying out of sight.

One evening, she had ventured out to the taproom where he was performing and nestled herself in a nook between the bar and the bathrooms. Hidden safely from his view, she had closed her eyes and listened to the music, her soul longing in vain to comfort the sorrow in his voice.

After a few minutes, she heard the familiar notes of a minor chord introducing the song they had written together, one that had been inspired by the poem she read that morning on the creek. In the end, she had stayed for only the first verse before her shoulders began to shake and she feared drawing attention. She left abruptly, the longing to mend his broken spirit overpowered by the desire to protect him from her festering presence.

On her best days, though, Jessica forced herself to play the part she had been assigned in the world, placing one foot in front of the other in an effort to simply do the next thing. Hiding behind her dry sense of humor, she much preferred to laugh. Deflecting depth with a wry comment, she could steer conversations from the dark places and pretend nothing was wrong. And maybe if she fooled others, she could deceive herself.

So, arming herself with sarcasm, she began building the walls that would keep her safe, would keep out the fears and uncertainties. From her steady perch within the fortified walls, she reasoned that if her happiness could not flow from a spring of its own, then she could pump it from a well of comparison. She hoped that by holding up her existence to others in harder circumstances, maybe, just maybe, she could rise above the gray balloon threatening to suffocate her.

Just look at Dan, she reminded herself. Each day he came into work looking more and more exhausted. Once he had even vented about his unhappy marriage and wayward children in the break room, which must have helped a little because he cheered up for a few weeks. But though he did not talk about it anymore, she could not help but notice that he looked unhappier with every passing day.

"Well, at least he'll stop by and say 'Hi' to you," Cathy had said quietly one afternoon when Jessica mentioned the change in his demeanor. "He doesn't really talk to me any more."

Jessica's life was much better than Dan's. She was wrestling a darkness inside herself, but his battle was apparently both within and without. Her life was better than Cathy's seemed to be, or even Stephanie's –

"Stephanie! Hi," she snaps from her thoughts at the sight of her coworker.

"Oh hey, Jessica, what are you shopping for?" she asks, and Jessica turns to the DVD toward her. "Oh, I didn't know you watched! Season 3? I was actually talking to Cathy about the show at work earlier. I'm almost done with the second season, and I am hooked!"

"I know, it's so good," Jessica agrees. "Except for how they wrote Josh out of the show halfway through Season 2 like that. That writing was terrible."

"Oh, you don't know?" Stephanie asks, going on to explain. "I read that the actor died of an overdose before they finished filming the season, so they just needed to get his character out of there pretty quick. I was reading something online that said they're actually thinking the actor might've done it on purpose."

"Really? Oh wow, that's so sad."

"I know, it's wild. I mean, if someone like that is having a hard time finding reasons to live, it sure doesn't leave much hope for the rest of us, does it?" Stephanie laughs.

"Not really," Jessica says with a sigh. "Thanks for that daily dose of inspiration."

Outside of the workplace, the two women do not share much common ground, so they continue to discuss the show in fits before lapsing into awkward silences. The rise and fall of their conversation is not wholly unlike the EKG of a dying person with no will to live who continues to be brought back by an overzealous attendant.

Finally, when they have exhausted all thoughts on the show, their exchange dies down. Neither woman is ready to leave, but neither has much left to say.

"Hey, so on an unrelated note," Stephanie changes the subject, "does Cathy seem okay to you?"

"What do you mean?" Jessica hasn't noticed anything different. "She seems alright to me."

"Well, just quieter I guess. She used to come around every afternoon – just 'Mother Cathy,' doing her rounds, checking on all her work children," Stephanie laughs. "She doesn't come around a whole lot now. I just didn't know if you've talked to her lately."

"No," Jessica admits, "but maybe her department's gotten busier with the merger. Or it could be her son – maybe he's struggling again. I thought I heard he was in rehab."

"Oh yeah, maybe. I feel like he already did a stint in rehab," Stephanie wonders aloud. "I know Cathy was trying to let him feel the weight of his decisions without letting him totally wreck his life."

"Sounds rough."

"Yeah, I'm never having kids. Anyway, she and Dan would sometimes come by in the afternoon so we could compare notes on the show, but they haven't in a while. I just didn't know if you knew anything."

"Nope," Jessica says. "Sure don't."

Stephanie glances up as a young woman approaches with her arms full of baby supplies. As she passes them, Stephanie and Jessica shoot each other knowing glances: the glazed expression, greasy ponytail, and gray sweatsuit all point to the natural downhill drift of a young mom in the wild. She carries herself like one who has simply given up – perhaps, more like one whose surrender was not accepted, who has been sent feebly back into the battle.

Her undignified appearance saves their dying discussion. After she walks by, the women cringe at each other as their conversation takes a cruel turn.

"Yikes," Stephanie scrunches up her nose and grits her teeth.

"She's seen better days," Jessica shudders. "At least, let's hope she has."

"She must have twenty kids at home to go out looking like that."

"Probably so. Girl, you got to work on your game face," Jessica whispers to the woman's back. "That look says the kids are winning." She mimics the young mom's exhausted expression, and they burst into muffled laughter, made all the more amusing by the necessity of keeping it quiet.

"I'm never having kids," Stephanie reiterates. "Never. Ever ever ever."

5

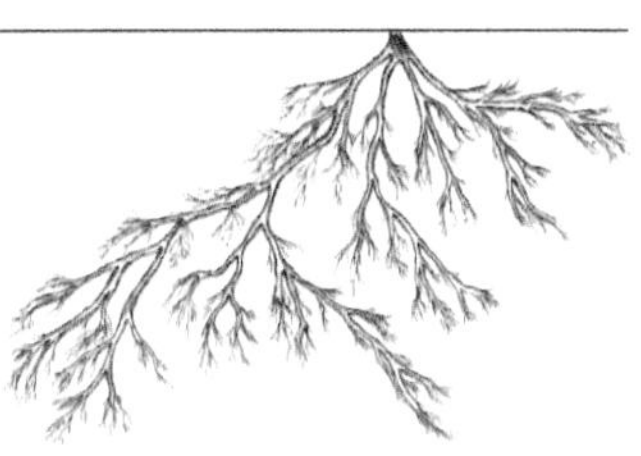

Baby Clothes

"Same," I say, shaking my head in disgust. "If I ever do have kids and you see me out looking like that, please just put me out of my misery." Stephanie sticks out her hand to shake on it. *It feels good to laugh like this again.* Even the guilt I feel as I watch our sagging target walk away is quickly squashed by my reassurance that I need this. The Dark simmers below, and I need to laugh today.

But the women do not realize that someone else needed to laugh, to resurface for air today. They have no idea that the spirit in gray sweats has troubles running far deeper than their opinions of her.

After many years of trying without success, there was a baby. Two months ago today, the doctor had confirmed that she and her husband were pregnant. Finally.

There were so many people to tell, so many friends with whom to celebrate. There were so many dates to be calculated and calendared, so many small decisions to be made. There were so many terrible smells in the fridge, and she spent many thankful mornings on her knees in the bathroom. The years of heartbreak and desperate prayer had culminated in a small blip on the sonogram – the appearance of a precious gift.

"Anna, for this child we prayed," he had cried. She agreed, and they planned a special way to surprise their unsuspecting parents. They spent the evening shopping for a baby book that would reveal their treasured secret. She narrowed the choices down to eight solid options, and he finalized the decision in a bracket-based competition based solely on "aesthetically pleasing book cover" and "lowest number of questions requiring a journaled response from Dad." Preference was given to the latter.

She had playfully punched his arm.

"What?" he asked as they walked to the front of the store. "I've got lots of stuff to do, and I can't spend the next nine months writing out my feelings." He flexed dramatically. "I'll be doing man things, like building the crib and stuff."

They made their purchase and headed out to dinner, where they spent the next two hours plotting out their big revelation. She jotted down a basic outline of their presentation on a notepad, assigning speaking parts and camera duties. Although she initially said they would need to practice their parts throughout the following week, in the end, they only managed to wait forty-eight hours before inviting their families for dinner. And when they arrived, Anna divulged the secret before they even sat down to eat.

"For this child we prayed," their families had cried. They agreed, and they imagined a future of ice cream dates and spoiled sleepovers.

"I'm thinking I'll go by Grandma Lou," her mother had announced two days later. "I had a Grandma Jodie, and I like the double names like that. Oh, but that might be too hard for the baby to say. Could you try to say it like a baby would?" She scrunched up her face as Anna made her attempt. "Hmm, that may be too tough. I should maybe do something like Nanna instead, though I'm not sure I could get used to that." In the end, she certainly could not and "Grandma Lou" began making earnest preparations for her new role.

Each night after dinner, Anna and her husband picked up their book of baby names and read entries aloud to each other for fun. She disqualified the ones that would not roll easily off her tongue in discipline, and he eliminated a few due to obscene initials or unpleasant rhyming capabilities. They quickly discovered that their vastly different styles did not often overlap.

"I think something free-spirited can be fun," Anna asserted almost every night as she tried various combinations. "Not everyone has to be named after a fancy little French prince," she teased him. "Like what about 'Dahlia Sage' for a girl?"

"Now what kind of bacteria is that?"

"Come on, be serious for just a minute – "

"Sounds like you could die from it," he said simply, and although they both laughed at his joke, the name was never mentioned again.

Each night, they added to their list of "Not-Completely-Hated" name options in a notebook and walked to the little bedroom at the end of the hall that was to become their favorite place in their home. They took measurements and bought magazines full of nursery ideas, leaping wholeheartedly into the preparations. She dug through the old trunk in the garage and brought out the newborn outfit they had purchased wistfully on their second anniversary, the outfit she had since feared was doomed to live in the garage forever.

But after the many years of trying with this one success, there was now no baby. Three weeks ago today, their doctor confirmed that although there had been a heartbeat, there was now no sign of life.

"For this child we prayed," they cried to the doctor. She apologized, and they spent the next half hour plotting the vulgar logistics of the greatest loss they had ever experienced. Carrying her broken heart in unsteady hands, Anna's mind drifted away in search of a safe place to stash it, to hide it away until she had more time to process the news. With great effort, she forced herself to return to the sterile little room where the doctor was speaking, discussing her immediate concerns and recommendations for mitigating the risk to Anna.

The pendulum had swung too fast, and her mind could scarcely comprehend the flood of new emotions. After struggling with infertility for years, Anna had clung to the sonogram as their guarantee of safe passage. She had seen the picture and loved the form. She had heaved her breakfast daily. She had never even considered the possibility that her due date could arrive empty-handed.

She spent the next weeks wrestling internally with questions for which she had no answers, only rounds of anxiety that eventually gave way to fitful sleep. Dreams of her bright future, which only days before had ventured boldly into the unknown, now hid from their own shadows. She tried to coax them from the corners and send them back out into the world – one which now looked far more untrustworthy – but they refused to go.

She spent the next weeks wrestling with her body's physical reaction to the loss, completely unprepared as the joyful indications of her pregnancy betrayed her with painful reminders of her loss. In the cruelest perversion, the fridge continued to nauseate her, and she spent many miserable mornings on her knees in the bathroom.

She had never before understood what a comprehensive loss it was, losing a baby. No one ever talked about it. She had thought miscarriages just happened, an unhappy but passive transition as what was to be became what no longer was, all before it was ever born. She was shocked as her unprepared heart continued to break over and over again, barraged by the relentless efforts her body made in its ugly struggle to right itself again, to regain its composure.

She spent the next weeks wrestling to recover joy. The loss of this child did not simply set her back a few months to the previous state of being childless. Somehow the having, if only for a moment, made the not-having far less bearable than it had been three months ago. Her work lost its purpose, her relationships lost their charm, and her world lost its color.

"Anna," her husband asked after dinner a week later, "we don't have to talk about it now, but can you let me know sometime what you want me to do with the crib? You want me to take it down and put it in the garage? Or we can sell it?"

She began to cry and nodded before changing her mind.

"I don't know if I'm ready yet."

"That's fine. We can figure it out when you are. But I think I'm good to get it out whenever you are."

"Is it bothering you?" Anna asked him.

"No, not really. There's just a lot of stuff around the house, you know? Like if we could paint over the walls and put some of it away, it wouldn't be such a constant reminder."

"Is that what you want though? Because it was real, babe. We'll meet him or her some day…just not now." Anna began to cry.

"Yeah, I know," he said as he rose to get her a tissue, "but sometimes it feels like a tough trade-off between honoring the baby's memory in our home and trying to avoid the ghost in the hallway." He stopped and shook his head. "No, not a ghost, but – "

"No, I know what you mean," Anna said. She appreciated her husband's honesty. Although she felt a steady desire to dignify the child's existence, she was determined not to allow their different responses to grief to tear them apart.

She spent the next weeks wrestling with her God. *For this child we prayed.* Over the years, Anna's struggle with infertility had refined her faith, as she fought to submit her heart to the Scriptures she was struggling to believe. God called Himself a "loving Father," and she could certainly see evidence of His goodness in her circumstances. But for years, she had continued to watch others receive the gift for which she herself had pleaded. Even less-deserving parents – those who abused or neglected their kids – received the blessings without even asking. She tried not to be jealous, not to ask those questions. She struggled to view God as the good Giver, instead of regarding Him like an aging Santa who, in the early stages of dementia, has forgotten which child asked for which gift and so doles them out at random.

Initially, it had been so logical to ask Him for the gifts because He said to ask. Then it felt so natural to thank Him for the seeming answer to those prayers because He said to enjoy the gifts with thankfulness. But now, she did not know how to talk to Him. *How does the Father, who says He loves to shower good gifts on those He loves, decide to give and then take away? And how can anyone choose to praise the One who snatches back blessings from His children?* And moreover, Anna often wondered if she was even allowed to ask.

The knowledge of a supervised universe had been a comfort to her before, just as a young child accepts the exchange of freedom for protection under the watchful eye of his teacher on the playground. But this new doubt about the intentions of the Supervisor unsettled her. She tried to pray, but she could not form any words. And when she was alone and the words began to converge into accusations, she was afraid to voice them.

"But I don't think it's wrong to tell God exactly how you feel," her best friend had acknowledged quietly just last week. They had been working side-by-side in the kitchen, preparing to watch the first football game of the season with their families. It was good to be reminded, and Bella's mom would know.

"One thing I'm learning is that God gets it. That as the Trinity – Father, Son, and Holy Spirit – He's a lot easier to relate to on a bunch of different levels."

Anna had laughed, "I can honestly say that's not a thought that's ever crossed my mind. Do tell."

"Well, God as Father God, you know, is this supreme being," Bella's mom opened a bag of chips and sampled a couple. "Making sure they're not poison," she joked. "He has all this power. He's mighty and sovereign over everything. And I love having an 'in' with someone that powerful, that big," she said, waving another chip through the air as if outlining His immense form.

"Sure," Anna nodded along but could not suppress her doubts about a big God who plucks gifts out of the hands of the people He claims to love. She finished stirring the spinach dip and grabbed some vegetables from the fridge. "Where do you keep your cutting board again?"

"Over there, second drawer from the wall," Bella's mom pointed, as she continued. "But He's not only this huge being. He's also this emotional dad who has to watch His son suffer because the sinful world's such a messed up place. And it's all broken and evil's squeezing His breath away, and your beautiful, amazing daughter won't ever get a fair shake at life by no fault of her own…Well, I guess I'm not talking about God anymore, am I?" she had admitted apologetically. "Would you stir those meatballs on the stove for me?"

"Yep, I'm on it. So you said the whole Trinity's involved – what about the other two?"

"Okay, then you have Jesus, and He has to suffer for sins He didn't commit. Like for you," she had turned to address Anna, and her voice faltered slightly, "it's encouraging to know Jesus can relate to your pain, which resulted from sin in general, not like it's the consequence of your personal sin." Anna had nodded. She knew this was true even though her heart, wishing desperately to find and fix the cause of their infertility, occasionally struck at her with accusations.

"And Jesus knows what it's like to feel abandoned by God the Father. Because all along, God's been proudly paving the way for Jesus in His ministry, even announcing audibly to the crowds, 'This is my son. I love him.' Like a very obvious connection between the two of them," Bella's mom illustrated by waving a stick of celery between two invisible beings in the kitchen before taking a bite. Anna smiled at the irony of the scene.

"What? Do not judge me, Anna. Celery could be poisoned, too – you just never know. You have to sample it all," she laughed. "So, anyway, God has been following Jesus around and bragging about Him, but then when life actually gets hard and Jesus's friends can't even stay awake to pray with him on the worst night of his life…like when our friends aren't there when we need them to be – sorry, that was back to me again," Bella's mom took a moment to collect her thoughts before continuing.

"So His friends let Him down, and He's there dying on the cross under the weight of sin that's not even His. And He's yelling out for Father God, the same Father who's always been so publicly proud of Him and communicated so freely with Him. But God doesn't answer. It's just quiet, like, where is God? Like when I'm pouring my heart out, and it's just silence on the other end, even when I'm praying with all my guts."

Anna, who had stopped chopping carrots, looked up with a wrinkled nose and glassy eyes. Bella's mom had ventured dangerously close to her own questions, and Anna wondered how her friend could live with a God who was so disconnected from her pain. She nodded but did not speak, fearing the tears she could not stop once they began.

"Anyway," Bella's mom shrugged, "it means something that the Bible then calls Jesus our great high priest, like He's made it His personal job to take our requests to the Father. It helps to know that my prayers, as honest and unbecoming as they can be sometimes, are being carried to the Father in the hands of someone who knows exactly what it's like to feel alone, crushed under the weight of the pain and – "

"But doesn't it bother you?" Anna stopped her, and they both turned from their work to focus on the conversation.

"Which part?"

"Well, you talk about God the Father being totally sovereign, but if He's as powerful as He claims to be, then doesn't it bother you that He lets really painful things filter straight through His hands to hurt us?" Anna asked, frustrated to hear her own voice intensifying as she struggled to restrain it. This question, which had been plaguing her mind but catching in her throat, forced its way into the conversation.

"Yes, it does," Bella's mom said quietly. "If we're being totally honest, it does. I don't understand it. But personally, I take a lot of comfort in knowing that everything broke when sin entered the world. And the brokenness had no place in God's perfect original design," Bella's mom said. "When I read my Bible, God talks a lot about hating sin for how it's destroying His creation and longing to bring His justice to make the world right again. And I know it's as personal for Him as it is for me – no one surrenders their child that easily. It does help, knowing that it's a part of God's mission to fight back sin's effects on Bella's life."

"But how? Like in what ways is that even possible here on earth?" Anna blurted out. She was immediately embarrassed of her bluntness. "I'm so sorry – I'm not trying to be rude, but I just need to know."

Bella's mom understood the struggle and dismissed the offense with a wave of her hand.

"Well, for starters," she began, "I know that it grieves God's heart that Bella gets frustrated when she can't catch on as quickly as other kids. And I know that His wrath is provoked, even more than mine is, when girls at school are mean. And, I'll be honest, I want to hurt them. Like *hurt* hurt them, Anna," she clenched her fists, "when they mess with her. But – "

A timer on the oven sounded, and she paused as she glanced around, trying to remember why she had set an alarm.

"I swear, I'm losing my mind," she laughed as she rolled her eyes. "Oh, I think that's for the rolls. Do you see my potholders anywhere?" Anna pointed to the kitchen table.

"Okay. So, where was I again?"

"You were talking about hurting children," Anna laughed, "but saying how God gets mad too – "

"Oh right. Yes, I think it just helps me to know He sees how crippled we are and how messed up our world is, and He mourns but not powerlessly like I have to mourn. In the end, He's going to break the power of sin and disease as He restores all of creation to the way it's supposed to be. Even though I know Bella is perfect and complete, one day God is going to show everyone she is by breaking the chains limiting her body. Anyway, I don't know if any of that helps you. But it gives me a lot of hope."

Thinking back, Anna did not know if it had helped or not. But it had been good to have an honest conversation, to see and name the pain. Many of her other friends did not know how to interact with her, first with her infertility and now with the loss.

"The heart is a funny thing, isn't it?" she had recently remarked to her husband. "Seeing their ultrasound pictures, I'm so excited for Bethany and Rick. I can't even imagine how adorable that little baby will be if he looks anything like them. Bethany tells me her news, and I am absolutely thrilled for them."

"Yeah, I'm happy for them," he had said, slipping his arms around her waist. "But if that kid gets Rick's nose or his stubborn streak, they're going to be in trouble."

She smiled but brushed quickly past his comment.

"And then I get in my car, shut off the radio, and ride home in silence. I get in the shower and sit down and just cry," she continued, resting her head on his shoulder. "I am completely happy for them, and it breaks my heart to the core at the same time. Like that could've been me. What if that's never me? You'd think those emotions would be mutually exclusive, but it's surprising how easy it is to both deeply thank God and also tear my heart out at the same time over the same news."

He nodded.

"For sure. The heart is a," he said, clearing the lump in his throat, "a very funny thing indeed. It's a weird land to be living in."

It had been nice of Bethany to invite her to the baby shower, and Anna is grateful to be included. But she rushes to finish her shopping as she feels the tears lining up to make their entrance. Maybe in the future she will be embarrassed to go out like this again, but as she carries her secret through the store, it feels profane: Here she is, still disoriented from the loss of the best thing that ever happened to her, walking past the shampoo. She is vaguely aware of other shoppers judging her appearance, but today she cannot care.

Still, she has picked out a thoughtful gift. Diapers, pacifiers, a toy, a book, an outfit – one of each little thing on the registry. Every time, she purchases more than she should for a baby shower, the gifts thoughtful and extravagant. And with each one, Anna writes the young mom a heartfelt card about the blessings of parenthood:

"…God has given you this amazing gift, one little proof that 'the steadfast love of the Lord endures forever.' Some days, it'll look like this miraculous child and beautiful golden sunsets. And some days, it'll look like the trying of your faith in the form of messes, meltdowns, and general mayhem. But they're all still aspects of that steadfast love of the Lord that never ceases, that gives the heart what it needs and not necessarily always what it wants," the notes read, and she writes them as much for the mothers as she does for herself.

She has put off writing Bethany's card for a few days now, but maybe she will write it this afternoon after she wraps the presents. Or maybe tomorrow. She sniffs back the emotion. *Yes, probably tomorrow.*

As she hurries toward the checkout line, she drops the pack of diapers, and a well-dressed woman of about sixty stoops to pick it up, helping restore the balance of her load. Anna blushes as she thanks the woman for her help.

"Oh yes, I remember those days. Enjoy them," the woman offers with a smile, as she steps into line with her box of bandages.

Fearing the onslaught of tears any minute, Anna follows the woman in the clumsy dance of two people who have already parted ways but continue to walk in the same direction. *What I wouldn't give to be buying a box of Band-Aids*, Anna reflects, *to care for pains that sit merely on the surface of the body.*

6

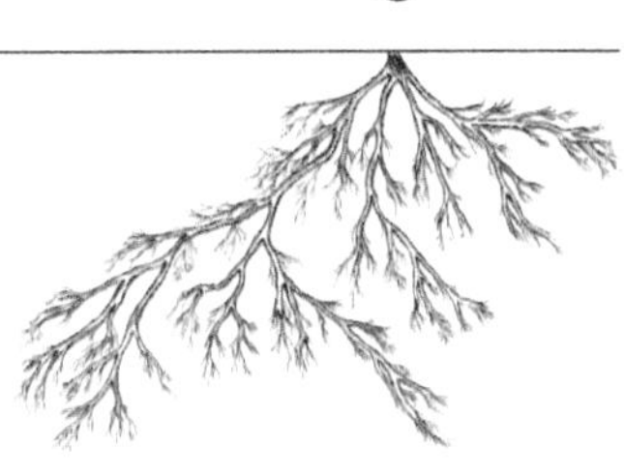

Bandages

Diapers, a toy, a book, some pacifiers, an outfit.

It's too much, I tell myself. *Just give a normal, reasonable gift. No need to go overboard.*

But reason never rules this argument – fear does, every time. *What if I never have to purchase these things for myself? What if I never get the chance to read a bedtime story, to pick out clothes for the day?* So, each time, I buy one of everything. It may be the last time I buy any of it.

Feeling the tears begin to converge, I turn my attention to the woman who helped me pick up the diapers.

"Thank you," she says to the cashier before her attention darts to a small boy with dark hair pulled neatly into cornrow braids. He has wandered over to look at postcards in a rack beside the door. "Oh honey, you can't just take those – you have to buy them." She leaves her bag of bandages on the checkout counter as she moves toward him.

"He knows," his mother says, stepping forward from behind me. "I let him look through them while we're waiting in line. He always puts them back when he's done looking."

"Oh, of course," the woman concedes a small step before plunging ahead, oblivious to the line forming behind her. "He's adorable."

She turns her smile upon the boy, who looks to be about ten years old.

"I'll bet you play basketball, don't you?" she ventures. I wish she wouldn't keep trying to force conversation, each attempt at dialogue teetering on the edge of the offensive. I feel my shoulders relax when the boy nods.

She continues, "Yes, I thought so. I see you out playing in the park with your little friends sometimes when I'm out walking."

The boy turns to look at his mom with a question, but she refuses to answer and directs him back to the woman. "I've got my own hoop in the drive. I don't really go to the park."

"Oh, in your own driveway? Well then, I'm sure you're very good. Your mom and dad must be very proud of you."

"Umm," he begins haltingly, "yeah. My mom, yes ma'am."

"Mmmm," she nods knowingly, as if the parts are all snapping expectedly into place like the precise pieces of an expensive model car kit. *Absent father.* Like she knows this story, has seen it repeated over and over again. "Of course, I see."

"There's nothing to see," his mother says, her hands beckoning her son back to her side. "I'm not sure what you're insinuating, but his daddy's not gone because he's black. He's gone because he passed three years ago, and we miss him everyday."

"Well, excuse me," the woman says loudly in surprise. She looks from the little boy to his mother. "I'm so sorry for your loss. Well, but I would never…I certainly never said – " she stumbles over her defense. Finally, with a great huff, the woman retrieves her bag from the checkout counter and hurries out the door.

"It's fine, baby," the woman turns back to her boy and nods toward the postcards. "You've got just as much right to look through those as anybody."

The conflict over, I feel myself relax as I load the last of my gifts onto the conveyor belt. Awkward as that conversation was, I feel a guilty appreciation for its ability to pull me outside of myself.

But as the embarrassed woman rushes from the store, the others do not realize she is walking toward her car almost as quickly as she is running from her past.

Valerie had grown up in a house that never was a home, never was a place of security. She slept in a dark room with peeling yellow wallpaper, sharing it – and almost everything she owned – with her younger sister.

Their father, bent low by the sins of his youth, never quite recovered after his best friend was thrown from the car after a night of heavy drinking, their last night together. Though her father was a broken man, he didn't carry himself as a lowly one. It was as if all the shattered pieces of him had healed back stronger, hardened like bone after the accident. Although the bottle had taken what was left of his self-respect, he returned to it time and again, dousing himself feverishly in its offer of amnesia. The drink did not make any demands of his conscience until it wore off, at which point he could quickly whisk himself away again as he emptied his trouble over the heads of his cowering wife and daughters.

When they met, Valerie's mom had loved his gruff persona and hoped to nurse him back to humanness with her love. Indeed, when he was sober, his residual guilt after an eruption twisted him inside out, made him uncomfortably kind and beholden. Valerie's mom had nearly left many times – but couldn't for his kindness and need, his lavish penance, his heartfelt apologies at odd hours of the morning. The yearnings that had snapped inside of him were so frayed and tangled that his wife was unable to weave them back together. So instead, she spent the better part of her days trying to piece together a shelter that would bear the brunt of his outbursts against her and the girls.

Early in school, Valerie and her sister learned to lie. They often stayed up late into the night weaving their stories together into a sensible whole. The bruises, the unexplained absences, the missing homework…they collaborated and schemed and, by their stories, proclaimed a reasonable alternative to their circumstances. Valerie could not admit to herself, let alone her classmates, that her father was little more than the mean man who lived in their home and often hurt them.

She had met Dale in the seventh grade almost fifty years ago. Chubby Dale, who was bullied by the other boys but who took notice where others had been too preoccupied. And as he heard, he started to unweave the existence she had so deliberately constructed. He began asking questions and following the logic of her explanations, calling out the inconsistencies as he uncovered them. One morning on the playground, he had motioned to Valerie from under the slide using their secret sign language.

"I've been thinking about what you said," he began as she came to sit in the shade beside him. "Your dad is abusing you and your sister. We should tell someone and get help." *Abuse.* Chubby Dale, finally naming the offense, finally acknowledging its wrongness.

In eighth grade, Chubby Dale gave her his family's telephone number and asked her to call anytime, day or night.

In tenth grade, Chubby Dale rode past her house at nine o'clock each night and watched for two flashes of her bedroom light, the signal that all was well.

In twelfth grade, Dale gave her a key to his house and told her she was always welcome.

After his second year of college, Dale asked her to move in with him.

Now, one ceremony, two kids, and almost four decades later, Dale asked Valerie if she might be too involved in their children's lives. Both William and Lynnette were now in their late thirties, and Dale warned that her advice did not always land as she intended. But, Valerie rationalized, every time she granted them the freedom to make their own decisions, they chose wrong. William had already been married once (*far too young*) and now had plans to move back into his parents' basement while he finalized the end of his second marriage (*I told him it wouldn't last*).

And Lynnette. *Oh Lynnette.* She and her mother had had their squabbles back when all of Valerie's friends were wrangling their teenage daughters. At the time, Valerie welcomed the opportunity to commiserate with her peers, often lamenting that raising teenagers is like caring for a wounded feral cat –

"You try to help, you get bit," she loved to say. "You try to fix the wound, you get bit. They start to purr and you think it's safe to talk to them, you get bit. Heaven forbid you have to get them to the doctor. Why, they'll take your hand clean off."

Even easygoing William had not been exempt during those teen years, which never seemed to end until Valerie felt the gradual, unfamiliar presence of peace and realized the season had changed. But Lynnette was different than her older brother in that she had never outgrown it. And Valerie continued to approach her daughter with a metaphorical net and long leather gloves and, therefore, found the anticipated feral cat in her traps, laid though they were with good intentions. So now, they spoke a few times every month, just long enough to catch up but never long enough to disagree. They still had not found a way to come back from that.

Valerie had last seen her daughter about two months ago when Lynnette stopped by so Dale could hear a strange screech her engine made. As Dale was checking under the hood, William called to ask if he could bring some boxes to store in the basement, and they suddenly found themselves in the position to eat dinner together as a family again, just like old times.

Somewhere between the salad and the main course, Valerie had turned to her son.

"William, I wonder if you might take up walking again. Those pounds around the middle can be very tough to lose if you let them linger."

He laughed nervously and nodded along. "I suppose I should, but I've been saying that for over a year now."

"Mom, that's so rude!" Lynnette interjected. "Can't you just let him live his life?"

"Well, excuse me!" Valerie exclaimed. "I apologize for being an attentive mom who doesn't want my son to die of a heart condition."

"I'm right here," William offered, but neither his mother nor his sister, for all their concern, could hear him.

"Here you go again, and I'm just so sick of it," Lynnette began.

"You just pick and pick and pick. Nothing's ever good enough. No grades, no choices, nothing we do ever lives up to the life you pictured for – "

"Well now, Lynnette, I have never… I only want what's best for you. End of story."

Lynnette shoved her chair back and slapped the tabletop as she prepared to present her case.

"No ma'am," Valerie said, "That's it – end of conversation." She waved her hand back and forth as though shooing that course of conversation from the room. Lynnette followed it out.

Later that night, Valerie replayed the conversation in her mind as she got ready for bed. Dale came to their room nearly two hours later to find his wife in tears, sitting at her vanity and removing what was left of her makeup.

"Why do they hate me?" she whispered, wiping her eyes with a rough swipe of her hand. "Why does everyone always hate me?"

"Oh Val, you know how Lynnette is. She'll cool off and realize she didn't – "

"Am I really so terrible to be around?" Valerie's voice was clipped by a sob that struggled free and burst into the room. Overcome, she covered her face with both hands, crying into her palms as her shoulders slumped under the grief of rejection.

Dale had always appreciated Valerie's strength, her independent nature wrought by the darkness of a childhood requiring that she take care of herself. She was resilient and capable, never pilfering from forward progress in the name of backward grief as she buried her suffering. She had cried before him only a handful of times in their marriage, and though he hated to see her agony, Dale treasured the moments he could see the cracks in her facade. Valerie's cool restraint commanded Dale's respect, but her humanity endeared her to him.

As she sat in her mismatched pajamas, mascara pooling on her cheeks before it snaked its way down her face, Dale pitied her, this giant of a woman brought low at the word of her child. For but a moment the veil was lifted, and Dale realized it was the pain, rather than the pride, of the mother bearing down on her children. He held her as she passed the rest of her heartache, felt it drain the strength from her body, and then tucked her into bed.

The next morning, Dale turned over in bed and immediately sensed Valerie's absence. He sat up abruptly, gaining his bearings as he looked for his wife. To his surprise, he saw her sitting at the vanity again – showered and dressed, hair brushed, makeup applied, putting in an earring.

"Good morning," he ventured. He searched her face for the broken woman who had collapsed into bed the night before but could find no trace. "Did you sleep okay?"

"Yes," she said curtly. "I'm not sure what came over me last night, but the rest certainly helped." She stood and walked to the closet.

"Well, I think maybe you were just hur–"

"How could Lynnette say that? How dare she?" Valerie stormed, slamming the closet door. "Sits at my table and tells me I pick at her and hate everything she does?" *I'm sorry I'm a mom who's involved, who cares about her kids' lives,* she fumed. *I suppose she'd like it better if I spent my nights checked out, chugging beers, just beating the tar out of the dog.*

Dale reminded her simply, "Lynnette knows you don't hate everything she does. We share our stories and beg them not to make our mistakes, but at the end of the day, they're just going to do what they're going to do." He shrugged. "Maybe even make our same mistakes, Val. Maybe it's best not to interfere, if only to protect the relationsh–"

"I am not a meddling mother," Valerie interrupted, ignoring her husband's position where it crossed her own. "I'm a good many things, but I am certainly not that."

On the morning of her ninth birthday, Valerie had found a small birthday card on the kitchen table. Inside were two crisp dollar bills. Her father's handwriting scrawled, "It's a special day today, so we're celebrating with ice cream tonight. Big girls buy their own." The bills made Valerie smile all day, whispering a secret to her each time she slipped her hand into her pocket.

At recess that afternoon, she pulled the money out of her pocket to show a friend. Word of her wealth spread among her classmates quicker than the flu, and soon a small crowd had gathered around her in admiration.

"Heard you got some money," Nicole said breathlessly, taking a break from a game of tag. Valerie never played tag with them. She typically avoided any interactions with Nicole and her friends after several stern warnings from her father about what he would do to her if he ever caught her socializing with "the likes of those instead of keeping to our own kind."

"Yeah, two dollars for ice cream tonight," Valerie exclaimed, proudly showing her the bills.

"Wow, you're rich! Alicia," Nicole yelled across the playground. "Look! Valerie got two dollars for her birthday."

Alicia joined the marveling throng.

The overflow of attention distracted Valerie from her father's warning. When the girls invited Valerie to play tag with them, she happily joined and was so engrossed in their game that she never saw her father's car drive past slowly at first or saw it circle back and park across the street until after they went back to class.

When Valerie and her sister leapt from the bus that afternoon, they raced home with an excitement they never felt as they neared the house. Her father was sitting on the front steps waiting for them, and Valerie wrestled the bills from her pocket as she ran toward him.

"Time for ice cream?" she asked. "I'm ready to pay."

She was unprepared for the clumsy hand that landed heavily across her left ear. Knocked off balance, she cried out as she tumbled to the ground. Her mother rushed to the screened door, but Valerie's father growled at her to get back inside. He shoved Valerie's sister through the door and ordered their mother to take her back to the bedroom. He snatched the money out of Valerie's hands and lurched for her sleeve, pulling her inside the house.

"Daddy?" She screamed in confusion as she struggled to free herself, but she was no match for his drunken strength as he slammed her to the kitchen floor.

"It's my birthday, please, it's my birthday," she cried over and over again as she curled up her body, locking her arms around her head to absorb the torrent of blows.

When his rage had burned itself out, he finally slurred, "Hope your little game o' tag was worth it today." *Oh*, Valerie realized, *because I played tag with the black girls*. "What have I told you time and time again?" he quizzed her.

"We keep to our own kind," she mumbled between sobs.

"Louder til you get it," he demanded.

"We keep to our own kind."

"'Cause if you don't, you lose your dollars every time."

"Yes sir."

"Yes sir," he laughed as he stumbled back outside, the screen door slamming behind him.

As she limped down the hallway to her room, her mother scrambled from the back bedroom and took Valerie in her arms. After cleaning the blood from her nose and lip, her mother sat Valerie on the bed and handed her a small present. Valerie slowly tore the paper open to find a yellow bracelet and matching necklace.

"Thank you," she told her mother and set it aside. Her mother smiled weakly and walked down the hall to begin tidying up the kitchen's evidence of the lopsided struggle. Valerie followed her like a shadow on the wall.

"There now, let's make you some birthday dinner," her mother offered. "Breakfast for dinner? Your favorite?"

Valerie nodded and sat at the table, watching her mother fry the bacon and cook the eggs in the leftover grease. When the meal was ready, Valerie nibbled a small piece of bacon, but the salt stung her lip, and she excused herself to go read in her room.

The day's exhaustion overcame her, and her head bobbed as she struggled through her book. Valerie had fallen into a thick sleep when her father opened the bedroom door shortly after midnight.

"Girls?" he whispered, switching on their light. "Girls, wake up. I think we owe Valerie some ice cream."

Valerie eyed him warily as she sat up in bed, but he wouldn't make eye contact with her and instead nudged her sister awake. *Ice cream in the middle of the night?* Even though he was doubling back and trying to make things right, she dared not cross him again.

"Yeah?" He tried to excite the girls for their midnight snack. "I learned one time how you can make homemade ice cream in the freezer. Let's make some – sound good?"

His sleepy children had made homemade ice cream before, but they obediently followed him down the hall. In the kitchen, he gathered cream, salt, and ice. Valerie noticed he forgot to add sugar, but she said nothing as he mixed two bags, one for Valerie and one for her sister, and placed them in the freezer.

For twenty minutes, they sat at the kitchen table as their father tried to make conversation, attempting to redo Valerie's birthday without acknowledging its reality. When the timer sounded, he grabbed the bags from the freezer and handed them to the girls.

"It doesn't... I don't," her sister fumbled before stating quietly, "I'm not hungry."

Valerie tried it. It tasted exactly as she had expected, given the ingredients – a bag of frozen, salty cream.

But choking it down, Valerie ate the entire bag's worth. That night, she concluded that if a promise was to be fulfilled, she had to do it herself. If a dream was ever to be achieved, it would only be through her own choices and hard work. Relying on others had only ever hurt her in the end.

Nicole found Valerie sitting alone on the playground the next day.

"Hey, how was that ice cream last night?"

Valerie glared at her.

"Worst ice cream I ever had," she said and pushed past Nicole as she walked back toward the school.

Heading to her car, Valerie pulls a bandage from the box and opens it. She sliced her hand earlier this afternoon while cutting vegetables for William's salad. *Always taking care of that boy who can't seem to take care of himself.* It had happened hours ago, but the persistent little slit keeps popping open. Placing the bandage carefully on the inconvenient cut between her knuckles, Valerie's mind shifts the blame until the accusation stops stinging. She grows indignant at the woman's words. *How could she judge me? Pastor Wilson just talked about this at our church last Sunday. Didn't I write down what he said? Didn't I nod in agreement?*

Right before the altar call last week, Pastor Wilson had sat down on the edge of the stage, feet dangling as he spoke to the congregation with an uncharacteristic informality.

"Can we just talk?" he asked. "I'm tired, ya'll. I turned on my television this past week, and I'm just overwhelmed – there's so much hate and brokenness everywhere. There's so much anger, so many hurting people fighting tooth and nail to hold the torch of justice themselves. It's exhausting, you know?"

Valerie had glanced at Dale, who was nodding along, his eyes fixed on their pastor. She wished William and Lynnette could hear this, but they had stopped coming to church with their parents years ago. *That could be why their lives don't look like they want them to*, she reasoned. *It really could be.*

"And it's got me thinking this week," Pastor Wilson continued, "that maybe a God who's not only loving but also just is exactly the sweet relief this world is thirsting for. God isn't just a factory of love and happy feelings, although that's what people think they want Him to be – the Giver of Blessings, no strings attached. But I look at how frustrated everyone is – it's like we're being crushed under the weight of a world that rides on our own ability to administer justice.

"Think of the freedom that comes with knowing God is going to make everything right in the end. That He calls us to bring His kingdom here on earth and get as far as we can in the spheres where He's placed us, but that in the end, He has said, 'Vengeance is mine; I shall repay.' He's seen the deeds done in secret and known the hearts of those who have done them in public, and our God refuses to be silenced as He rehearses the names of those He will avenge. Doesn't that bring freedom, cast off the weight?"

The weight. Valerie nodded absentmindedly to the question, as her mind ventured off to other ways she could help William lose those extra pounds. *I'll stock the basement fridge with vegetables – that'd be a good start.*

"But ya'll, listen up, this is so important," Pastor Wilson pleaded with such conviction that Valerie snapped back to the sermon. "Now don't think I'm suggesting we ditch responsibility for our effort, basically resigning ourselves and saying 'God will work it out in the end, so I don't need to do anything just now.' Why? Because that blatantly disregards how Jesus taught us to pray when He said, 'Your kingdom come, your will be done on earth as it is in Heaven.'"

An infant began to cry in the next row, and Valerie wished the Stewarts would just put their baby in the nursery. This happened every Sunday, and they always waited until the last possible moment to leave the room. She glanced back over her shoulder before turning back to the pastor.

"So let me ask you, church," he was saying. "If God's plan for His kingdom is to redeem this place so there's no more sorrow, no more pain, no more injustice, no more evil spreading over the earth – just how might God's people proceed in response?" He stood and walked back to the podium to retrieve his Bible.

"Intentionally, that's how." Pastor Wilson ran his finger over the worn leather binding as he continued. Valerie had written down the final part as he rattled it off, getting louder and louder in a crescendo until his voice broke. He whispered his final point before turning and walking quietly offstage:

> *Where the conversations are polarizing, engage them.*
> *Where the souls are invisible, see them.*
> *Where the hearts are hurting, mend them.*
> *Where the system is broken, fix it.*
> *Where the heart is convicted, humble it.*

Now, almost a week later, Valerie envisions Pastor Wilson with his legs swinging as she nodded her agreement, and her face flushes with anger at the woman's words. *You can't even talk to people anymore without someone getting offended. She wants to talk about racism? She should've met my father. I'm not a racist – I don't even notice skin color.* She excuses herself in her own mind, deflecting the accusation without stopping to consider its full weight. She does not take it carefully in her hands, running her fingers appraisingly over its threads or shifting the cloth in the light to better examine the quality of the fabric. Instead, she quickly sets it aside.

Of course, I'm not overbearing.

Of course, I'm not prejudiced.

"Of all the things I could be accused of," she chuckles aloud to hide her embarrassment, "I am certainly not that."

And so she was, as are a great many of those who refuse to look, thereby depriving themselves of the chance to see.

7

Milk and Cereal

I shake my head in disbelief as I dial Dale's number, smoothing the bandage as it buckles when I bend my hand. I can already hear the incredulity in his voice when he learns the allegations. In spite of the confrontation, I smile to myself as I approach my unreasonably sporty little Nissan, a Christmas surprise from Dale last year. *Well, at least Dale still loves me.*

I pass an older gentleman who looks through me as he walks toward the store with his fingers wrapped awkwardly around the handle of a milk jug and a plastic bag with a box of cereal inside. In his other hand, he holds a small black keychain.

I toss my purse and the bag into the passenger seat before sliding inside. I look in my rearview mirror just as the old man walks back past my car, pausing occasionally to look down at his hand before surveying the lot again. Apparently, he has lost his vehicle somewhere in the parking lot and is trying to find it using the alarm button on his fob.

Flustered, he wanders once more toward the far corner of the parking lot. He nods a quick greeting to a young woman he recognizes from another life as she climbs into a blue truck before he turns and walks back toward the front of the store again. He frantically mashes the button again, but to no avail. *It is happening again.* He tries to minimize the number of trips he takes to the store for this very reason.

Of course, there are the other things like misplacing his list or forgetting the pin number for his debit card. But this latest development makes his failings all the more conspicuous and threatens to topple his self-respect.

Throughout his life, he had been a natural leader, bold in instruction yet humble in tone. He had managed his shop and served his family for the better part of fifty years, offering guidance to improve the lives of those who welcomed his advice.

Unfortunately, as he aged, his mind did him the disservice of not vacating all at once. Some minds deteriorate rather quickly, graciously allowing those with dissolving dignity to remain blissfully unaware of its passing. His mind, however, remained sharp enough to make special note of the moments it failed and to bring them to his attention, like a cat who continues to drag dead mice to the back door in search of praise. It became particularly painful when his employees began to disregard his advice as the musings of an old man rather than the wisdom of a more experienced individual.

"Excuse me, sir?"

He jumps, called back to his parking lot dilemma.

"Excuse me, did you forget where you parked?" The young woman pulls alongside him in her blue pickup. "I do that all the time. What kind of car are you looking for?"

Alice. She looks just like her. It was just like Alice to help him, to protect him and pull him back from the verge of humiliation. How he missed her! She had made it easy to be a man, had helped him climb when he was climbing and had helped him back down into old age. Life was not as much fun without her – a little less steady, a little more scary. *Has he still not spoken?*

"Oh! I'm, I'm so sorry. You remind me so much of someone I used to know. It's uncanny," he recovers, his face reddening in splotches that creep out to his ears. "I'm sure it's around here somewhere. It's a, a white car. It's a white Dodge car." *Why could he not remember the model of the car he had been driving for eight years?* "I hate when I forget where I parked - happens, uh, a lot these days. It's rough getting old."

She graciously smoothes out the wrinkles of his speech.

"I do it all the time," she offers, "and I'm only thirty-five. Hop in, and let's drive through the lot to find it."

Somehow that comment always makes it worse, although he appreciates her attempt at encouragement. *That's one problem with this younger generation* – they keep downplaying things, trying to make him feel normal when he knows this is not normal. If they could just let him be old, let his memory be failing without writing him off entirely. Sure, he knows his mind is declining, but he's still sharp much of the time with wisdom to share if anyone wanted to hear it.

And he has stories – good ones, too. He had sacrificed his youth for his country, serving proudly in the days when the greater good was valued over individual comfort. He had served alongside honorable men, eaten unrecognizable meals with them, drawn on their strength when he wanted to run.

Those days had rattled him with fear, but he had taken pride in doing his job well. But although they had been assured this work was for the ultimate good, he still had to push back the confusion each time he saw the great cost of the "good." By the age of twenty-five, he had seen more death and lived through more adventure than the forty-year-old employees in his shop today, the ones who roll their eyes at each other when he drones on about his experience in the war or his love for his country.

After the war, he met Alice by chance when he stopped at the ice cream parlor one afternoon. She was everything pure and bright to his sad, disillusioned mind. Her cheerful greeting caught his attention, but it was her peaceful spirit that convinced him she would always be a safe place for his experience and pain. Over the course of the next few months, with the intuitive use of her words and her silence, she soothed the places that hurt his soul.

For her part, Alice loved the depth in his eyes. She loved the way his smile did not take pleasure for granted, but rather collected each one and turned it over and over in his hands, thankful for its healing presence. Where she would see a pretty meadow from the car window, he would stop the car and get out and walk among the flowers, running his hands over their cheerful faces with a childlike appreciation. He would get on his knees and collect the prettiest daisies, threading their stems together into a makeshift bouquet.

"Come on, let's go," she would plead, "we're going to be late – this is not the time to be picking flowers."

And he would smile and rise, presenting her with the bouquet in an elaborate show. As she looked down at the bundle of daisies in her hands, each time – without fail – she would find one ugly, drooping flower among the bunch, one that did not fit with the rest. She would look up at him with a furrowed brow.

"Because," he would say to her unspoken question, "that's real life."

They had not been going steady very long before they fell into the comfortable recognition that she would be his lifeline and he would be her anchor til death did them part. As a step in that direction, he got down on one knee in that ice cream parlor nine months after they first met, and they were married a few months later.

Their first year of marriage drifted by with the ease of an autumn leaf floating on the river, as conversations every evening stoked a bright fullness in their relationship. Each discovery brought new intimacy as they found themselves more fully known and loved. Everything was as it should be.

The next few years brimmed with fun adventures – a new home to enjoy, new babies to love, and a new business to run. He observed Alice, appreciated her dedication as she invested late nights and early mornings in their family. His heart swelled with pride as she alternately played with and disciplined the children according to their need. She was strong, with solid opinions that sharpened his own – his capable partner in business and in life.

But as they worked together toward their common goals, they

gradually forgot how to be together, to rest in each other's company. Early on, they had taken great care in arranging the store and spent many a happy afternoon dusting and rearranging their wares without distraction. Now those distractions were usually boisterous, often dirty, and routinely picked up dead animals.

As they corralled the children and managed their growing business, they found less time to speak to each other, and when they took time for conversation, harsh words crept in where harmony had always been. Afraid of this dangerous shift in their marriage and unsure of the best way to close the distance, Alice tried to hold him to herself on a tether of control, becoming critical of the things she had always loved about him.

"Could you pick up some flour so I can make bread with supper?" she had asked him one afternoon.

"I will, but I've got to say a few words over the squirrel. I think one of the dogs got him. The kids found his body in the yard this morning and made up a little box for his burial. They've asked me to see to it he has a proper funeral," he explained, offering, "I'll go get some right after that."

"It's not even a real funeral," she insisted with frustration. "It's a squirrel, *a squirrel.* Please just do the service after you get the flour."

"But, Alice, it's not just a squirrel to the kids. They want him properly laid to rest, and I intend to help them. The bread can still be ready in time for supper. Just give me a few minutes to finish this."

She disapproved of the ways he spent his time, bossed him as if he were one of her children. She hoped to pull him, harnessed by her criticism, back onto the path she desperately wanted to walk with him. He felt her critiques keenly and began to withdraw to safer ground. It was an ominous cycle that made each desperately unhappy, though neither could see a way of escape.

One night, he found her in tears as she brushed her hair before bed.

"We've been married for ten years today," she said flatly. "Happy anniversary. We made it."

He had forgotten their anniversary. The monumental day had

passed like any other – an afternoon sandwiched between a morning and an evening. Alice generally didn't make a big deal of holidays, but anniversaries were different – they were a celebration of the hard work they had poured into their marriage thus far, and when lavishly observed, were an investment in the next year's happiness. Until now, he had never spared an expense in honoring the day. But things at the shop had been so busy recently.

"Oh no, I am so sorry – " he began.

"I guess I saw it coming," she cut him off. "What are we even doing? We're running this shop together, we're raising a family together. But we don't ever just spend time together like we used to," she cried. "Why should today be special when none of the other days are? It shouldn't have surprised me, but still – "

"Now, Alice, don't turn this into any more than it is," he said. Of course, today he'd made a critical mistake. Of course, they'd been busy and lost touch lately. But all families have rough seasons. *And,* he noted bitterly to himself, *she hadn't mentioned their anniversary today either, until she wielded it now as a weapon.*

"Any more than it is?" Alice burst into tears and told him exactly what it was. He stood staring at the floor, listening to her words as she verbally dismantled all that she had devoted her life to protecting. She got into bed, rolled to face the wall, and cried bitterly as she mourned both the years that had driven them apart and her words which now would fix them there.

He cleared his throat and quietly said, "If that's how you feel," then opened the door and walked to his truck. Though at first it would not crank, he refused to go back inside to finish the fight. After fifteen minutes of struggle, the engine finally yielded and sputtered to life. He drove dark back roads throughout the night, preparing his words and steeling his heart for the inevitable confrontation. He was only a few miles from home when his truck shuddered and then coasted to a stop. He pounded the steering wheel, cursing first his truck for its betrayal, then himself for the empty fuel tank. He kicked the door open and slammed it behind him as he started walking.

Trudging through the fields before sunrise, he rehearsed her faults, fine-tuning his monologue as he prepared for the clash. As he gained confidence from the evidence mounting against her, he suddenly remembered a verse his mother had made him memorize decades ago. *Man, that was a lifetime ago when we were kids.* His sister had knocked his bicycle into a puddle, so he threw mud on her and called her a dirty name. She tattled on him, and they had both been ordered to memorize a passage from the Proverbs. *Why would that surface now? This situation is totally different. How did it even go again?* It began to come back to his mind:

> *A soft answer turneth away wrath: but grievous words*
> *   stir up anger.*
> *The tongue of the wise useth knowledge aright: but*
> *   the mouth of fools poureth out foolishness.*
> *The eyes of the LORD are in every place, beholding the*
> *   evil and the good.*

"Probably best you look away, God," he said to no one in particular, "this may get ugly."

But as he walked on, those verses began to perforate his arguments, and he struggled to keep his points in order. He wasn't sure if it was the beautiful sunrise, the brisk early morning exercise, or those pointed words from the King James version, but as he strode for home, his anger dissolved as a new feeling emerged in its place. He had spent the last couple of years watching his marriage swirl as the bathwater does before it goes down the drain – slowly at first, then faster and faster and faster.

No more, he decided as he walked through the fields. *I'm plugging the tub.* Armed with this new resolve, he abandoned his interest in the easy road, the one tempting him to walk away from the fight and keep on walking. As he passed through the fields that morning, he picked a handful of daisies like he had done so often during their early days.

When he got home, he placed the flowers on the kitchen table with a note that said, "Since the war, I haven't had anything to fight, mostly thanks to you. But somewhere along the way, I drew up battle lines with you on the other side. I don't really know how we ended up here, but starting today, I want to be on your side again. I want to fight for us." Then he slipped out the front door again to open the store before she woke up.

When she walked into the kitchen that morning, she glanced apprehensively at the bouquet, which evoked so many memories of their early years. She stepped closer for a better look. There, in amongst the beautiful flowers, was a hideously withered one. It was the one for which she was looking.

"Because that's real life," she smiled as the tears began to form. "I'm ready."

It was the biggest fight of their lives – the daily falling in and out of love, the constant swelling and humbling of selves, the moment-by-moment strain of choosing to honor each other. But they fought it, and in the end, they won. Many times, they had feared they might not. But as she lay still, waiting peacefully as the sickness nudged her further into eternity, Alice's final words to him were, "We made it. Come soon." And that lovely smile.

It was the proudest victory of his life. He had learned in the war what it meant to serve the greater good, to offer oneself for the masses. But he learned in his marriage what it meant to sacrifice himself for another individual, one who often opposed or hurt him. In the end, the victory over the struggle brought a fulfillment only known by those who have experienced it.

During their first year of marriage, he thought he knew what it was to be fully known and fully loved. But as the years passed, Alice had shown him more and more what it meant to be fully –

"Well not fully, old man," Carl had said to him again last week when he dropped by for lunch. "We can't ever fully, fully know people this side of heaven even if we truly, truly love them. But the deeper we know them, the deeper we can love them. Like with Judy, I kept thinking we'd arrived and then ten years later I'd look back and see we hadn't even started yet." Carl had been stopping by more frequently since Judy's passing six months ago.

"I know exactly what you mean. Alice knew me so much better than anyone this side of heaven and chose to love me anyway. Even when she shouldn't have," he added with a laugh. "And it just kept getting better as we learned more about each other. I didn't even realize it at the time, that the limits kept shifting until I would look back – "

"Well, it's like an asymptote, you know," Carl interjected.

"Like a what?" he scowled, annoyed at the interruption when he was talking about Alice.

"An asymptote. It's a math thing," Carl replied. *Thank goodness Judy saw him under that brain. Seems the more Carl loves his math, the less people love him. Must be like a reverse asymptote*, he chuckled to himself before focusing again on his friend, who had taken up his professorial role as though he had never retired.

"…A line in math where the values continue to approach that number but never actually get there, all the way out to infinity – "

"Carl, I got to be honest with you, that doesn't mean a thing to me."

"Well stick with me, and you might learn something yet. It's complicated mathematics but applies to life as well," Carl squinted his eyes, sensing his friend's frustration and trying to explain himself both fully and quickly.

"I didn't invest my time in complicated mathematics – "

"It's basically a math scenario for, let's see," Carl floundered about for an example. "Okay. So say you buy a bone for your favorite dog. But you have this rule that you'll move it halfway to him every ten minutes. Well, all day into the rest of eternity you're moving it toward him, but it never actually gets all the way there, even though it's constantly getting closer to him all the time."

"Sounds to me like I don't actually love my dog, like I'm torturing him for fun. Slightly reminiscent of a conversation we're having – "

"But," Carl cut him off again, "you get the picture. An asymptote is the math version, but in a relationship, if that line is perfect knowledge of and perfect love for another person, you can see how we never get all the way there in this world, messed up as it is. But even as damaged as things are, we can – and you and Alice did – get closer and closer to it every day."

"Mhmm. And when I get to heaven – "

"Well don't be rushing that, old man. But yes, when we get there, all the earthly limits are gone, and we'll actually be able to fully know and fully love each other. Heaven really is going to be amazing."

Scanning back through the memories, the dark times making the bright spots shine that much more brilliantly, he realized how much Alice really had seen him, in all of his ugliness, strengths, insecurities, fears, successes, humiliations. And with all that she had, she had loved him anyway – not fully, but truly, as close as a man could hope for on earth. *Heaven is going to be amazing,* he thought, *but I sure hope God checks all that complicated mathematics stuff at the gate.*

But when he forgets where he parked, it's as if none of these things matter. No one wants to hear the ramblings of an old man. His thoughts often tumble forth as insight interlaced with a meandering story that culminates in a forgotten ending. Great wisdom can still be found, but it has to be mined with a little more patience and dedication. *But maybe that's the point. You can't get to the gold without all the grimy layers of life sticking to it. Just like Alice would say, "Gold doesn't float and growth isn't free."*

"That's it," he says to the woman, pointing out the windshield. "Right here, this white one. I wasn't even close this time." *I must've walked right past it.* "Thanks so much for your help."

"I was happy to," she says as she watches him climb slowly from the truck. "And next time you'll have to help me find mine. Seriously, it happens to me once every few months. Hope you have a good day."

He forces a smile and waves before turning away.

As he pulls the keys from his pocket, a young man with a

bouquet of flowers flings open the door of the florist's shop next to the supermarket. The old man nods to him as he strides past, whistling a catchy tune. Daisies. *Alice sure loved those daisies.*

8

A Bouquet of Daisies

"Daisies are a good choice. You enjoy her," I tell him with all the gravity I can muster after another embarrassing incident. "Time flies, and I had fifty-five years. Just don't blink."

"I've got to win her heart first," he admits, "but I figure these can't hurt."

"They were my wife's favorite," I tell him. "Good luck, son."

That's why I still put the daisies in the vase every Sunday. Early in our marriage, they had been a picture of my love for her. Then after that morning walk through the fields, daisies became a picture of the commitment we made to each other. Now, they are simply a celebration of the promise we worked out in the end; they –

I forgot to get the flowers! I rage at myself. I knew I was supposed to get more than milk and cereal. *Oh well, I'll ask Rachel to bring some when she comes tomorrow to check in for the week. No sense in leaving that silly white Dodge car alone again so soon.*

My eyes follow the young suitor, strutting off to his big moment. *You're in for quite an adventure, son. Get ready.*

And he is, as ready as he will ever be.

The first date had gone well enough – at least they both acknowledged the awkwardness. Charlie hated first dates. He hated the sense of evaluation that gave him no chance to let his guard down, no chance to find comfort in either the conversations or the silences. Thankfully, she openly admitted to feeling that way, too. Her outspoken demeanor that cheerfully yielded to a ready smile reminded him of his mom, how she had been before her mind had started unraveling. He found both some peace and some pain in the familiarity.

His mom had always been brilliant and ambitious, even before his dad died. But after that, it seemed like something had ruptured inside her head, the beginnings of a mudslide that would eventually pull the foundations from under her feet. Something in her mind broke that morning but healed back incorrectly, channeling her restless energy into eccentric pursuits. As he got older, Charlie attempted to reason with her, but she fought him, and her mind often flitted away to a realm where her husband still walked beside her.

Charlie couldn't blame her. His dad had always been the fun one, the eager parent who put down his work to play with his son on the floor. He was the one who wrestled, who pranked, who bestowed the love of music.

Charlie still had the photograph on his nightstand. It was, in fact, the only photo he displayed in his apartment. In the picture, his mom had captured one instance of a recurring occasion in their home, when Paul took Charlie into the den for one of their "Boys-Only Jam Sessions." Charlie was three years old at the time of the photograph and not much taller than the ukulele in his scrawny arms. His father was kneeling beside him holding a guitar, and they were making faces at each other. At the time, each thought they would have a lifetime to make memories like these.

Then, on the morning they got the call, his dad had passed away, but in a way, Charlie's mom had, too. But she did so much more gradually, and her body continued to live. Charlie was not sure which was harder. His mother's continued physical existence, though broken, would not grant him either the license to mourn or the comfort of her presence. The headstone on his father's grave gave him the permission he needed to grieve, but it served as the cold reminder of his dad's absence. Charlie's father would never come to a gig or help him with his tie. And today, he could use some help with the latter.

Second dates were always his least favorite. He had had three of them, two of which were also coincidentally last dates. So in his mind, they had major implications for the longevity of a relationship.

He knew, of course, that survival of the second date was no guarantee of forever. He and Jessica had dated for two years, happily for eleven months before her depression began to pull her away.

Charlie had been reluctant to introduce Jessica to his mom, fearing the uncomfortable collision of his worlds. But when he was finally ready and mentioned the idea, Jessica shook her head and told him she was not prepared to take that step, probably never would be.

"What? Why not?" he had pressed.

"It honestly has nothing to do with you," she sighed. "It's just me, I can't get there."

He jerked his head back with a frown.

"What are you saying?"

"It's just this heaviness in me. I'm so tired of fighting, and you don't deserve this. You need someone who will be a strong support for you. I can't even be that for myself – much less for you – right now. And I might never be."

"We can get through it. I know it will be a struggle, but I'm all in," he had reassured her, moving next to her on the couch. "Let me be here for you. I can be strong enough for the both of us," he said, grabbing her hand to pull her back from the ledge.

"Charlie, we've tried, and it's not working." She began to cry. "We're both miserable – me, because I can't shake this, and you, because you can't even see what we're fighting against. So we just end up hurting each other. Maybe it's my fault, maybe it's nobody's, but this just isn't working. I love you, but I can't even carry my own weight in this," she said, pulling her hand away as she rose to leave.

"Then I will. All you have to do is let me in, Jess, just let me help," he pleaded. She struggled to pull on her jacket.

"I can't," she cried, pressing her frail arm into a tangled sleeve. "I know you can, Charlie, and you would, but I can't."

Jessica cried harder as she bitterly thrashed her arm inside the uncooperative sleeve. Charlie reached inside it to straighten the twisted parts, as he gladly would have done for her heart if she would let him. Determined to fix the mess, he followed helplessly as she gathered her things, like a child at the beach trying in vain to protect a beloved sand castle against the battering of the waves. He shook his head in disbelief as she turned down the hallway, paused at the door, and then showed herself out.

In the following weeks, she stopped returning his calls and avoided his attempts to see her. Finally, Charlie took the only action within his power – bothersome in its cloak of passivity – and gave up, offering her the space she had requested. Releasing the castle to the waves, he walked away. Just as he had when his mom refused to remain among the living, when her tired mind preferred to converse with her late husband instead of her living son.

Charlie would never choose to give up; he would always fight for them, even fight with them. *How is it that he could just walk away from the two most important women in his world? They had let him go. So why did he feel so helpless, somehow so guilty?*

But relationships require two invested individuals; one person can't hold it all together. Both must look each other in the eye, say the truthful things that must be said, and wrestle through the mess to find a solution. Each must commit to the struggle because walking away is not an option.

If that quarter is left in the gumball machine, Charlie had learned, *someone will inevitably twist the handle – they'll spend that quarter every single time.* Jessica had done so, opting to trade that of lasting value for that of temporary comfort. With his mom, Charlie was not sure which of them had made the decision – all he knew is that he had looked down one day, and the quarter was gone.

It had been four years since Jessica left, and Charlie was reluctant to begin again. He had always assumed that when she was able to climb out of the Darkness, they would find each other again. But, as far as he knew, she had never climbed out nor had she come looking for him.

And he had tried to make himself findable. Jessica had loved watching him perform his songs, and she had not only inspired them but also understood them. When she walked away, he plunged himself deeper into his music. Under the searching eye of his piano, he could channel the feelings plaguing his heart into melodies expressing his jumbled thoughts. Although initially his father's music had died with him, Charlie found it again in the piano late at night, singing the grief his heart could not resolve to the bar stools who could not comprehend. Late into the night, he poured his sorrow into the microphone, hoping, always hoping, that one day she would return to complete the ballads which never quite found their resolution without her.

But she had never come. Jessica made no effort to contact him, and he wondered at her silence. *At the very least, I'd want to know that she's doing alright. Does she care how I'm handling things? Did she ever care?*

He had assumed that he would always love her, always prop her up as the unattainable standard to disqualify any who would follow. And for the first year after she left, he continued to idolize her. The happy memories swelled in his mind to crowd out reality so that even Jessica herself, on returning to his world, would be found inadequate. But, as expected by all except those who are suffering, time did ease the pain and bring new clarity.

As a young boy, Charlie had a favorite song which the local radio station played frequently. His mother showed him how to record it on a cassette tape, and after capturing it, he played it back constantly, listening to it for hours each day. The words didn't make sense to his eleven-year-old mind, but the haunting melody and the raw voice moved his heart. Young Charlie determined he would learn to play it on his guitar.

But as he set out to learn the song's intricacies, he found, to his dismay, that it followed a very basic chord progression, one that he could play with very little practice. Armed with only four chords and his own voice, he could reproduce both the music and the timbre very quickly, to the wonder of his mother.

But instead of encouraging his efforts, it had crushed him, reducing the lofty to the level of the ordinary. The magic of the song disappeared when he realized it could be recreated by a little boy with a cheap guitar on the front steps. Charlie, like the rest of mankind, idolized the unattainable and disdained that which could be held in human hands. He picked a new favorite song, set aside his guitar, and began taking piano lessons.

Time began to fleck the gold foil from his memories of Jessica. He had loved and understood her, and she had done the same. On good days, she had shown him the ways the inner Darkness had stretched her soul as only pain can. He especially loved the moments when she laid down her defenses, putting away the sarcasm and the deflecting humor, and spoke from her heart. The internal struggle had given her a depth which profoundly influenced both his thinking and his music.

"Come here, listen to this," she had burst into his apartment one Saturday afternoon years ago, back before the Darkness had swept her away. "Have you ever heard of Matthew Arnold?"

"No, but welcome, and come on in. Who is he?"

"A poet from way back in the day. I randomly grabbed a book of his work at the library this morning and discovered an amazing poem. It's like it was written about today, even though it's ancient. Honestly, it's like it was written for me."

"Hmm," he said distractedly, but she ignored his indifference.

"It's long," she warned, opening the book. "But listen. It's good stuff –

> *Fate, which foresaw*
> *How frivolous a baby man would be –*
> *By what distractions he would be possess'd,*
> *How he would pour himself in every strife,*
> *And well-nigh change his own identity –*
> *That it might keep from his capricious play*

> *His genuine self, and force him to obey*
> *Even in his own despite his being's law,*
> *Bade through the deep recesses of our breast*
> *The unregarded river of our life*
> *Pursue with indiscernible flow its way;*
> *And that we should not see*
> *The buried stream, and seem to be*
> *Eddying at large in blind uncertainty,*
> *Though driving on with it eternally.*

"No Charlie, listen, it gets better," she reiterated when she saw him lean back and close his eyes.

"I am listening," he said. "Sometimes I listen better with my eyes closed."

"Yeah right," she laughed. "Sometimes you fall asleep better with your eyes closed. Listen to this next part –

> *But often, in the world's most crowded streets,*
> *But often, in the din of strife,*
> *There rises an unspeakable desire*
> *After the knowledge of our buried life;*
> *A thirst to spend our fire and restless force*
> *In tracking out our true, original course;*
> *A longing to inquire*
> *Into the mystery of this heart which beats*
> *So wild, so deep in us – to know*
> *Whence our lives come and where they go.*

"Doesn't that sound like what we were talking about the other day? Feeling torn between always keeping things light and sometimes just wanting to stop and be real a minute?"

"Yeah, I guess," he began.

"I just kept feeling like this was written for me. Like it's about me," she said, scanning the page. "Oh I love this part. Listen to this stanza –

Only – but this is rare –
When a belovèd hand is laid in ours,
When, jaded with the rush and glare
Of the interminable hours,
Our eyes can in another's eyes read clear,
When our world-deafen'd ear
Is by the tones of a loved voice caress'd –
A bolt is shot back somewhere in our breast,
And a lost pulse of feeling stirs again.
The eye sinks inward, and the heart lies plain,
And what we mean, we say, and what we would, we know.

"Charlie, isn't it beautiful?" She looked at him expectantly. "'The eye sinks inward and the heart lies plain' – I can't think of a better way to talk about love. You should put this in a song, seriously. It's so raw. And it's something people should hear."

"Slow down," he laughed and pulled her to him, but she pushed away, intent on the conversation.

"A bolt shot back? A lost pulse? People are craving this deep down, and the 'din' and the 'strife' and all the rest of it are wearing us out, maybe because we don't think anyone else feels it. I especially love the part where it says we mean what we say and the things we would say, we already know."

"Yeah, definitely," he agreed, struggling to rise to the level of her excitement. "But I'm glad this Arnold guy is dead because it sounds like you might be in love with him. It's a lot easier to compete when the other guy's dead."

When Jessica rolled her eyes, he admitted, "I'm just hearing all this for the first time and the words are pretty dated. But if you'll give me a minute, I'd like to read through it all." He took the book from her hands and whistled. "Boy, it's a long one."

Twenty minutes ticked past as he toiled through it while she searched his face. But once he saw through the archaic language, he turned to her excitedly.

"You're right. I really think this is something. Come here," he said, walking to his piano. "I've got an idea. Help me with this."

That night, they wrote lyrics for a new song, piecing together fragments from a nineteenth-century poem and contemporary hearts still crying out for the same. The song was one of those magical pieces which is stumbled upon and polished rather than plotted out and crafted. When they finished, Charlie took an astounded, humble pride in it, and it quickly became his most treasured piece. He wanted to name it "Jessica's Song," but she refused the honor, and in the end, they settled on "The Heart Cry of Mr. Arnold."

It was a favorite with the regulars at the bars he played, and he had performed it often while he and Jessica were dating. Then after she left, he sang it religiously, at the end of every show.

"My eye sinks inward and your heart lies plain," he would sing, the words seeping from his lips while a montage of memories scrolled across his mind.

Jessica had been an amazing woman, and he often wished to find her face in the crowd as he gazed out over an audience. But ever so slowly, the pedestal on which he had placed her descended until he was able to view her more truthfully. Although for years she had stood at a distance while Charlie saved her a seat beside him at the piano, she now no longer held him captive.

Instead, he goes out most nights, sitting comfortably on the bench alone as he sings to rooms full of people who love his music but do not understand his heart.

Well, not tonight. Tonight he has a second date with a girl who readily admits she has never heard of most of his heroes. Her resounding laugh made him cringe at first, but now he thinks he would like to hear it again. She's the first to confess there are bumps in her story and chips in her shell, but below the scratches he has observed, his eye catches a glimmer. *There is gold beneath.*

Whistling the melody of his newest song, he lays the daisies carefully on the floor of the passenger side. He glances at the man getting out of a truck in the spot beside him. The man makes eye contact and smiles, nodding along to the song. *They do love the music,* Charlie muses. This new tune ends with a dissonant chord, the kind that feels as though the melody has been carelessly abandoned in the middle, like a sneeze which builds and builds but never resolves. Sometimes when he sits at the piano, he feels a compulsion to grant his audience that finality they crave. But life doesn't always resolve the dissonant chords, and his honesty hangs in the balance. Each night he asks himself, *Should I sing the song for the people or for myself?*

Myself. He stops whistling where the song should end, resting in the tension of something both uncomfortable and true. The man raises his eyebrows.

"Not where I thought that was going," he says with a laugh.

Charlie smiles and admits, "Yeah, no one ever sees that coming. Don't know if that makes it good or bad."

"I don't know," the man replies. "But I liked it up to that part." *They always do.*

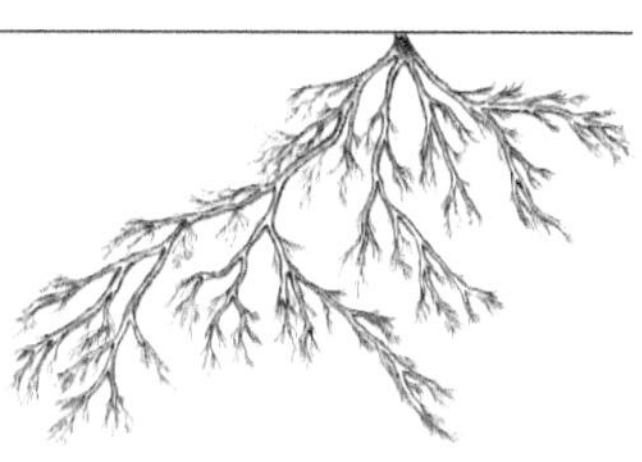

9

Cookies for Dessert

The crowds always love that resolution, hold their applause until they experience the closure. The bright melodies, the cheerful tunes, the consonant final fanfare that lulls them into believing all is right in the world. But sometimes I get tired of giving people what they want, filling my gigs with cheesy cover songs to keep hearts light. I get tired of glossing over reality when my heart just wants to say something true, tired of being forced to cheaply tie up loose ends and place a colorful bow on top.

I shrug and smile back at the man.

"That first part is really catchy though," he offers as he walks away. "The ending might just take me a minute to get used to." He's not trying to be rude, and I can appreciate the honesty.

As the man walks into the store, he catches the door for a nurse hurrying in on her way home from her shift. The dark smudges on her scrubs offer an incomplete commentary on the troubles of her day.

He initially considers trying to cheer her up, but instead he shrinks back, not from this particular nurse, but from a joke he heard at the office earlier today: *What do you call a panic at the hospital?* He can never outrun the shame, and the suffocating guilt stalks him always, lashing out today from an innocent exchange of corny jokes at work. Daily, he bears his remorse like a dull headache that never fully develops nor completely fades away.

As he holds the door, the nurse's listless expression asks an unspoken question, and he doesn't have the answer. So he scratches his forehead before smoothing his hand along his tired brow and says only, "After you."

After you. He sighs unhappily under the weight of his world, remembering the sunny day he had first met Elise – remembering how, for all his confidence, his voice had betrayed him as he opened the door for the most beautiful girl he'd ever seen. Those were the only two words he could scrounge up as he hunted for a better line, and his voice cracked on the first one.

"Thanks," she said and walked past him as if he was only holding open the door. He soon regained his composure and caught up to her, even joking about his treasonous voice that had let him down in his hour of need.

Her quick smile encouraged him, and he had asked her to lunch the following day. When the time arrived, he spent two and a half hours trying to impress her with stories of his friends and adventures and plans. At the end of the date, he told her he had had a wonderful time.

"And next time, maybe I'll even tell you a little about myself," she quipped, and Dan cringed when he realized he had never asked. But he recovered quickly.

"Next time? Are you asking me out again already?" He grinned. "A little forward, Elise, but I'm not opposed." Pompous though he was, Elise fell for him immediately, as had every girl before her.

A decorated college athlete, Dan boldly walked through the doors that his physical abilities opened for him, and he enjoyed popularity and friendships across many social circles. He could be found in the center of any room, his sarcasm drawing some people in and pushing others out with very little effort. Unlike those who found their worth in his current opinion of them, Dan rested confidently in his charm and never struggled for companionship, especially with women.

But for him, Elise was different. His friends assured him that she was only his latest challenge, another conquest for Dan the Man, but he disagreed. He respected Elise's thoughts about life and couldn't get enough of her presence.

"Come on, buddy, you're losing it," his teammates teased six months into the relationship. "Dan, it's Friday night. Remember what Friday nights are made of? You're seriously going to spend it watching a romantic comedy on a blanket in the park?"

"Whatever," he said, standing his ground though his face turned red. "You guys are just jealous."

"Well, looks like Dan is officially off the market," they laughed as they walked outside. "We'll make some memories for you then. Have fun with that movie, Domesticated Dan."

And he had good-naturedly laughed along, though he bristled at the inference.

"I will," he said. "See you tomorrow at that pick up game. Two o'clock, right? I'll pick you up off the floor after that, and we'll see who's domesticated."

"Keep telling yourself that. She's got you wrapped around her little finger," they taunted.

And she did. Elise smiled at others with a delicate curve of her lips, but she gave only Dan the depths of her heart. She confided her fears and insecurities in him, made him the trusted keeper of her dreams. And Dan became the man she saw in him, her faithful protector and most steadfast support.

Of course, they had heated disagreements and petty quarrels as they sanded down the uneven edges that had buckled in their coming together. In past relationships, Dan had never worked through the hard times, but it had never been worthwhile to him until now. On the night of their college graduation, he proposed to the woman who alone held his deepest secrets and gave him the privilege of bearing hers, too. They were married soon after.

For the honeymoon, they had saved their money so they could go on a cruise. Elise had never been on one before, but Dan promised her it would be "the adventure of a lifetime." Due to a conflict between Dan's new job and the cruise line schedule, however, they had to delay their adventure until six weeks after the wedding. Each morning, Dan announced the countdown and assured Elise the wait would be worth it.

Unfortunately, when the time came, Elise felt every movement of the ship and spent her entire time at sea trying to pretend that the disorienting, fluid floor was indeed a magical place to be. It was only when they arrived at a port and the seasickness followed her from the ship that Elise suspected another cause for her illness.

"Well, you never looked more beautiful. I'm almost tempted to propose all over again," Dan joked one afternoon when he returned from the deck to find his ailing wife huddled on the bathroom floor again.

"There's no going back now – we're having a baby together," she boldly announced, pleased to see his face pale until it matched the shade of her own.

After he had hugged her and kissed her on the cheek – "Girl, not on the mouth after what you've been up to!" – Dan admitted he was nervous to bring kids into the world, especially considering the horrible karma he had likely earned as a rambunctious child. But Elise's good karma seemed to negate his, and they floated into parenthood on peaceful waters.

After two years of marriage, Dan had established his career in a steady, albeit boring, full-time job. After five years, they settled into a new home. After seven years, Elise spent all of her energy caring for their four handsome boys. The days were long, and they collapsed into bed together each night in contented exhaustion.

One evening the boys organized a performance in the family room. They sold tickets to Dan and Elise and ushered them to their seats on the floor.

"A rip-off!" Dan whispered to his wife, who shushed him as she overexaggerated her excitement for what promised to be a wonderful show. Their oldest had assigned each of his brothers a part in the fifteen-minute production, culminating in his original song "I Pick Only Yellow Flowers." He belted out the lyrics as his brothers mimed their corresponding parts:

> *I pick only yellow flowers,*
> *Sam would pick a rose,*
> *Billy picked out super powers,*
> *But Thomas picks his nose.*

The boys collapsed in howls of laughter at their parents' shock as the youngest dug with his fingers in both nostrils. Elise gasped in horror, but Dan tried to disguise his laughter with a cough as he leapt to the makeshift stage to redirect the evening's entertainment. In the end, he failed, and the song became a family anthem that resounded throughout the evening and for years to come.

After fifteen years of marriage, things relaxed into a comfortable monotony. Dan had gained recognition at work and received a promotion that included a substantial pay raise. Elise went back to work part-time and took great pride in keeping a tidy office and an orderly home. The boys were an unruly bunch and did their part to counteract her work with their clutter. Although life lacked some of the adventure from their early days, the years were short, and both Dan and Elise rested happily in their life.

The boys had each inherited a generous helping of Dan's personality and a delightful piece of Elise's heart. And what they lacked in genetic giftings was carefully instilled by their parents, who beamed to see the boys blossom into kind, capable young men. Ever so slowly, Dan and Elise turned their gazes from each other and fixed them upon their children, into whom they poured the best of themselves.

They had put thousands of miles on their relationship and now enjoyed the ease with which their life flowed without requiring much maintenance. They basked in the fruits of their hard labor – rested in the shade of their peaceful home and glowed with pride as the boys excelled in their own realms.

After nineteen years of marriage, the ground trembled. Their oldest son had surrounded himself with rebellious friends who led him down dangerous roads. When two officers knocked on the door one morning, his parents were dismayed to learn of his wayward behavior, which threatened to capsize his promising future. His own welfare aside, his misconduct threatened to publicly embarrass his family, to uproot the graceful tree his parents had so carefully cultivated.

But neither Dan nor Elise cared about the tree – they cared about the boy. They had adored the happy child who picked only yellow flowers, who narrated each day with his endless chatter.

Even now, they loved him, though he most often appeared in the form of a defiant young man with an empty gaze, who was systematically working to disassemble himself, limb by limb. On rare occasions when light broke through the storms, he would laugh with his brothers. His dimples would reappear, and Dan and Elise would recognize the little boy who had organized family productions with his brothers in the living room. These moments passed so quickly that they wondered, each time, if it had not been simply a mirage, the hopeful flicker of their imaginations.

To see him not only so lost but so unhappy broke their hearts, but they disagreed about how to deal with him and how to bear their own feelings. Dan felt only a strong hand could call his son back to reality, and he often resorted to stern methods as he tried to help his flailing son regain his footing. Elise, on the other hand, believed the boy needed to feel understood, and she frequently reassured him of their open door and unconditional love. Each became irritated at the other's methods, just as they were disheartened at the failures of their own. But it was easier to blame each other than to watch their precious boy struggle while they looked on so helplessly.

The frequent, late night conversations wore them down as they tried, in vain, to reason with him. By the time they collapsed into bed each night, they had no energy left to offer each other. They often finished one argument with him only to walk down the hall and begin another in their own bedroom.

"He's just a boy, Dan. The things you say aren't wrong, but they always beat him up. He'll never come to us if he thinks we're out to get him. You're just pushing him away," Elise would scold.

"When I was his age," Dan would argue, his voice rising with resentment, "I had a job and a work ethic and a girlfriend. My old man was hard on me, but I stepped up, and I think I turned out alright. Coddling him isn't going to make him grow up and start acting like a man. It's just enabling him, handing him a blank check to go out and wreck his life."

Each tried to unearth those elusive magic words, the argument they had not yet found which would cut through the bitterness and finally reach their son. The pain ran so deep that silence brought the only reprieve. It became easier not to talk, at least not to talk about the central thing on each of their minds.

So it had not been apathy, nor was it a cruel, calculated misstep when Dan made his mistake. Perhaps it was only a thirst for distraction, for momentary happiness to numb the ever-present pain. It began at work one day, when Dan vented his frustration to some coworkers in the break room, just to speak his burden and find validation for his ideas. He had said too much, revealed more than he'd planned, and he regretted it.

But a few days later, Cathy had asked him if he was making any progress with his son. She was the office mom – "Mother Cathy," as Dan had nicknamed her for her hospitable ways – and she always stopped by his office in the afternoon on her way out, just to chat. She too had a headstrong adult son, her only keepsake from a marriage that had disintegrated around her. She understood Dan's inability to reconcile his dreams for his family with the life they now lived. When her world fell apart, Cathy had numbed the broken places by pouring all of her energy into her work family. Perhaps, she admitted, that's why she felt so guilty that her son eased his misery by pouring himself a glass every night, then another and another and another.

In the beginning, Cathy was simply a sounding board as Dan expressed his opinions about the situation and asked another woman's perspective. Their lunches increased in frequency.

Cathy became a confidante as he voiced his frustration with Elise. She understood his thoughts and affirmed him as he fought for his boy. She made Dan feel respected and appreciated like he had not been in a long time. In the end, Cathy became far more to Dan than he had ever planned and far more poisonous to his marriage than she had ever meant to be. The drift had been so gradual yet so great that he did not fall far when he met her after work one evening.

The thrill was over immediately. In his heart, Dan knew Cathy held not one sliver of the charm or ounce of the character of the woman who had already taken on his name, his faults, and his life. The temptation, which had looked like such a fresh and promising escape for his tortured mind, now revealed itself to be a cheap, unfulfilling substitute for the life he already had.

Crippled by guilt and longing for the steady, even difficult, life he had known before, Dan confessed his transgression to Elise the following week. He had never seen her cry so hard, and then she went silent, speaking to him only in front of the boys.

Counseling had helped to a degree. At least they were talking again. And Elise had admitted to the therapist that she was "still in it, at least for the kids." Elise loved those boys and would stay with Dan forever to keep their sons from feeling the slightest wobble of insecurity. But even if she could go on like this indefinitely, Dan knew he couldn't keep living under this miserable arrangement much longer.

He felt powerless. The counseling was not helping that. In delving to the depths of her pain, Elise unearthed years of hurt and anger with each session. This new injury had validated every old ache, which was now named, charged, and released venomously back into their marriage. It was as if the one act of yielding to temptation had forever stripped him of his footing in their household, of Elise's respect.

She was bent on extracting the proper, yet unspecified, amount of penance from him before offering forgiveness. It often seemed as though it was being dangled overhead, always just out of reach, and he never knew when she would want to revisit his shame.

Just last night, as he was reading in bed, Elise returned from the bathroom with a small card in her hand.

"Hey, get to a stopping point because I have something to show you."

"Okay," he said, "just got another page or so." He was struggling through *Letters to Theo*, the story of the failing and later famous artist Vincent van Gogh, told through Vincent's letters to his brother.

Although it was not a book Dan would normally choose to read, he had picked it up one afternoon after Sam brought it home to read for a school project. Fearing that squandered opportunities would send his second son down the path of the first, Dan seized the chance to connect, to "join my boy in his misery."

As the letters waded through van Gogh's big emotions, Dan had often skimmed over the pages with a disinterested sigh. But last night, as on very few occasions, Dan lingered over one of the sentences that caught his attention, sympathizing with the artist's lament.

"There may be a great fire in our soul," it read, "but no one ever comes to warm himself by it, all that passers-by can see is a little smoke coming out of the chimney, and they walk on."

You're a tormented little man, he said under his breath. *But I get what you're saying.*

Turning to Elise, he asked, "Okay, what you got?"

"You remember this?" She held up a picture. "It's been my bookmark for a long time. It's from our date right before the homecoming dance?"

He shook his head. "Was that the time we went out after midnight trying to find a corsage? Ended up making one with a dandelion or something?"

She laughed.

"No, this was the night you read the poem you wrote for me. Do you remember? It was so sweet, I had my roommate take a picture of us so I could always remember us that way."

Dan closed the book on his finger, marking his place so he could return to it later. He laughed and covered his eyes with his other hand.

"Oh no, you didn't tell her I wrote you a poem?"

"Well, I read it to her," she admitted with a smile. It felt like old times.

"Elise! You read it to her? I don't even remember what I wrote, but I bet it was a corny version of 'Roses are red' – "

"You don't remember what you wrote?" She drew back and looked at him.

"Of course not, that was years ago! How could I know what I wrote in a love poem back in college?"

"You're right – that was a long time ago," she said, her voice taking a colder tone. "I guess you probably wrote a bunch of them for the girls. That was a lifetime ago anyway, never mind."

Dan suddenly felt exposed. Her playfulness had disarmed him before she jabbed him with the painful reminder.

"Yeah," he said, feeling the accusation keenly. "I guess so." And as he said so, he withdrew his hand from the book, set it on the floor beside the bed, and turned over.

But that was last night. When he gets home this evening, she will be cooking dinner as he walks through the door. She will let him kiss her on the cheek as they call their children to the table for dinner. They will share stories from their days, disagree about how to load the dishwasher, put the younger children to bed, and withdraw to their own happy places.

She will open her book, immersing herself in an imaginary tale where love breaks down the walls of a guarded heart. He will fall asleep early, drifting off to a dream where his deepest sins have been erased and he can look Elise in the eye again. Where the eye sinks inward and the heart lies plain, perhaps even innocent.

Maybe one day we'll get there, they both think. But neither takes a step today.

He sets the package of cookies onto the conveyor belt and

sighs. The boys love these chocolate chip cookies. *That'll be a bright spot in the evening tonight –*

A sharp pain shoots up his right leg.

"Ah, watch out! That's my heel, guys," he lashes out irritably at the boys behind the shopping cart. "Some of us are just trying to shop in peace."

Immediately, he regrets his words. Their mother turns red and mumbles a hasty apology before herding her sons into another lane to make their purchase. As he pays for the cookies, Dan looks down, avoiding eye contact with the cashier as he pretends to search through his wallet for something he has lost. Something else he has lost.

"I don't need a bag. Thanks, have a good day," he mutters to the cashier as he grabs the cookies and walks toward the door.

When he looks up, he spots the nurse again, looking somehow less happy with her bag of groceries than she had looked before. *A mid-wife crisis.* It had been a harmless joke in the break room, but the rims of his tired eyes glow red. The misery is inescapable. The guilt lurks everywhere.

10

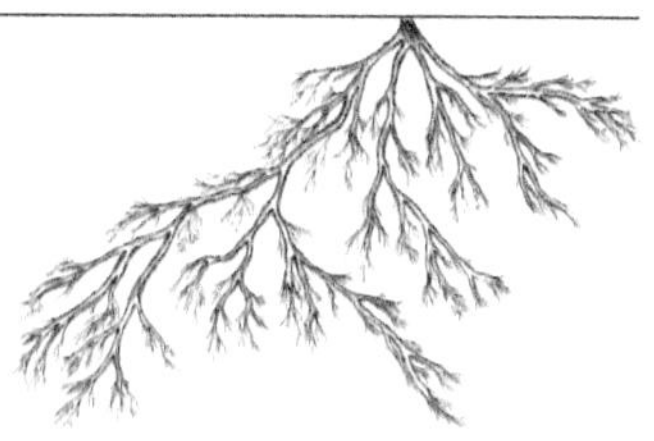

Toothpaste

"Rough day today," I say to the nurse as I get the door for her again, but it's only after she passes that I realize I offered it as a statement rather than a question.

"Thank you. Yes, you have no idea," she says, and I smile sympathetically because I just might. She shifts the grocery bag to hide the stains on her scrubs, as though she's embarrassed by the stories behind them. I look away, recognizing and granting her wish to avoid further conversation. *I feel the same way.*

But her silence has nothing to do with strangers in the grocery store. Her hectic day, with all of its remnants on her scrubs, is just another reminder of how different her life is from the way she had pictured it.

None of this had been part of the plan. She had dreamed big dreams, imagining her life as a spin-off of the hospital dramas on television. After spending several years gaining experience in the field, she had finally landed a job in the fast-paced emergency room, her first goal materializing. But the reality looked nothing like what she had envisioned. In her mind, she and her colleagues would work tirelessly to save lives together before going out for breakfast after a long shift. But life is not always considerate of the dreamers, and Rachel was often frustrated at the protocols stunting her ability to interact with her patients and the unspoken rules separating her from her coworkers.

There was an invisible curtain that isolated her. She had first noticed its presence in middle school, around the time kids begin noticing the differences amongst themselves and building their friendships accordingly. She didn't like music class, and she told the teacher so. She didn't like sleepover parties, and she told the girls in her class. She didn't like sitting alone at lunch, but this she told no one.

"Don't you want to invite any of the other girls from your class to go with us?" her mother had asked a few weeks before her eleventh birthday. "The zoo's a fun place, and you might enjoy it even more with a few friends."

Rachel considered the offer. She imagined the girls pairing off exclusively like they did in class, telling her to "shut up" like they did at lunch, hiding from her like they did at recess.

"No I don't want to. They're not my friends."

"Well, Rachel, maybe you just need to get to know them a little better. And this could be a fun way to do that."

"No, it's my birthday, and I don't want to," Rachel replied.

So she did not invite them, nor was she invited by them, nor did she tell anyone how it felt to be constantly stuck on the outside, peering in through dirty windows.

"She'll grow into it," her teachers had reassured her parents.

"She's so socially awkward," her classmates had said in college.

"She's an odd duck," the other nurses had said. "No idea how she got this job – she must know somebody." When she walked into the lounge at the end of her shift, Rachel noticed the furtive glances shooting around the room. As time passed and she failed to assimilate, the others grew bolder in their hostility, often making cruel comments at her expense.

Like hens, who peacefully coexist within the brood by uniting against the most vulnerable, Rachel's peers sacrificed her spirit for the harmony of the whole. The daily pecking wore her down. It had felt like a degrading surrender, the day she offered her resignation to the fast-paced world and redirected the course of her career.

Although home health had its share of benefits, the work felt demeaning at first – the baths, the bed pans, the feeding tubes. *If only they could see me now,* she mused miserably. She longed for the impressive world of work she had left behind, her mind painting misleading pictures of her days at the hospital.

As Rachel continued at her work, however, her heart began to change. Whereas she had dreaded going into the ER every day, she now woke with a sense of curiosity about her day, if not excitement for it. She not only took pride in improving her patients' lives in tangible ways, but she also looked forward to the conversations she would have with them. Her patients liked her as a person, and their joy in her company helped to soften her own insecurity and loneliness after the cancer broke her heart.

A few days ago, she had cried in the shower for the first time in three weeks. Most of the time, she could suppress her feelings, but some days the grief overtook her. A good cathartic cry usually provided some relief for the open wound on her heart which resolutely refused to scab, to give up.

When she got out of the shower, she had touched her puffy eyes before putting on her makeup and fixing her hair, with a quick glance at the mirror to confirm she was back in control. She didn't have to stay out very long anyway – that day, she had only one patient to see.

"Good morning," she greeted him as he pulled open the door.

"It is," he said happily and stood aside to welcome her into the crowded entryway. "I'm almost six feet above ground rather than six feet below. That's always a good day."

"Very true," she agreed. She did not acknowledge that he reported some version of this good news every week.

"Though, honestly, some days I'm just ready to go home to see Alice," he continued. "Now I don't think I'm even close to actually dying, so don't go looking all concerned. But my body is old, my mind is going, and some days I'm just really ready to go ahead and go on, too."

Not me. I haven't gotten to live, she thought. But she did love to hear him talk about Alice. Hearing their story gave Rachel hope that her own life could someday blossom into more than the broken dreams her heart refused to release.

Back when she was thirty-two, still working at the hospital, she had been engaged to a man who was several years younger. They had met at the birthday party of a mutual acquaintance. She was playing with the dog in the backyard instead of sitting around the campfire where the others were making s'mores. He made his way over to introduce himself and was unfazed by her awkward conversation.

"You don't have to stand here with me," she said after a quick handshake. "I much prefer dogs to people anyway." She shook her head in frustration at how the phrase sounded when she said it. "Not 'anyway,' but I do prefer dogs."

"No offense taken," he smiled. "I actually prefer dog people myself. They tend to be loyal and don't mind a mess. Can I throw one for him?"

She handed him the ball, pleased that he had chosen to stay with her, in spite of her. He stuck like no one ever had before, drawing back the heavy curtain and offering her entrance into the world of her peers. She looked forward to seeing him each day, and then one day, he surprised her with a ring.

But two short months after they announced their engagement, a routine visit to his doctor about some minor symptoms veered wildly off course. Within hours, he had follow-up appointments scheduled with two specialists. At each turn, the news darkened, and the prognosis was bleak.

They walked the grim gray hallways to sterile rooms, where doctors probed and prodded and pricked him.

"What am I, a pin cushion?" He winced but always tried to make Rachel smile.

The doctors scoured his body, looking deep within for some hint of hope. Or at least an absence of its opposite, which would declare hope the victor by forfeit. But Rachel's optimism dwindled each time the scans showed the masses spreading hungrily like a wildfire.

All of Rachel's training had prepared her to take care of someone else, never the other half of herself. She took the burden to be his strength and salvation upon herself, though it was much too heavy for her. At each appointment, she locked her heart outside the room, leaning into her medical training and making careful notes as his doctor suggested ways to ward off some of the pain.

At the end, she took several weeks off work to provide as much of his care as she could. With her breaking heart bound and silenced so she could perform her duties, Rachel numbed his pain in those final days, unable to take it from him any other way.

After the funeral, she had thrown herself back into her work, even more withdrawn than before.

"Poor thing, must still be in shock," hushed tones buzzed in the hallway.

"It's such a pity. He was actually a really nice guy," another of her coworkers whispered outside the bathroom door. "She won't ever find anyone else like him."

"Never would have put those two together, but I guess it worked somehow."

"I know. I never believed in soulmates, but – "

"Oh hey, Rachel."

She nodded at both of them. Before he lit up her world, Rachel felt she had nothing interesting to say to them. After he passed, she wanted to talk but didn't know how to begin. The others sensed there was something else to say but couldn't figure out what it was, so they excused themselves to return to their work. By their silence, they clipped the most beautiful wings, the ones he had given her.

That had been years ago, back in the harried days of late nights and long shifts and short conversations. Walking away from it had been hard, but looking back, Rachel could see that the change had been good for her. A fresh start with people who needed her help and enjoyed her presence.

"Just make sure when you pray for me," her patient had said, "that you tell God I'm ready to go see Alice."

She lurched back to the moment.

"I will," she said with a smile. "Tonight I'll tell Him just that."

But that night when she got into bed, the words still would not come. They had been evasive ever since they were powerless in their pleading. Sometimes she tried closing her eyes, but she always opened them again immediately – closing her eyes to pray did little more than shut them to the needs of the world. With this line of thinking, she hoisted a great load onto her shoulders, one she was never meant to carry.

As a young child one summer, she vacationed with her parents to the beach. While she couldn't remember much else about that trip, she often thought about a special father-daughter date on the last morning of their vacation. The evening before, they had walked the beach together looking for shells, crabs, and a perfect picnic place. Then, they prepared a meal that was to be their lunch the next day. Everything was carefully bundled and set aside to be packed in the morning.

Young Rachel was so excited she woke up before sunrise the next day and ran to wake her father. He laughed and explained that not only was it not lunch time, it was also not breakfast time, nor was it time to be awake. But her excitement was contagious, and in the end, they decided to make it a breakfast picnic.

After gathering all of their things, they headed down to the shore. As they walked along the water, her father carried their chairs, towels, shovel, bucket, and picnic lunch-breakfast in a cooler. At five years old, Rachel was anxious to exercise her independence, and she asked her father repeatedly to let her carry her own belongings.

"Honey, these are much too heavy for you," he had explained, adding cheerfully, "and besides, I'm happy to hold them for you."

"But I'm strong, and I can carry my chair, towel, shovel, and bucket," she had insisted. "They're my things."

"Rachel, they're pretty bulky, and I'm afraid you won't be able to hold it all. You could get tripped up because this chair is as big as you are, honey."

"Daddy, these are my things," she whined. "I want to carry them. I'll be so careful."

"Alright then, my dear," he had conceded. "Here are your things." And handing her the chair, towel, shovel, and bucket, he set off again toward the picnic spot they had scouted the evening before.

Stubbornly yet admirably, Rachel struggled along behind him over the sand. But as she walked, the chair became too heavy for her, and she had to leave it behind. Her towel unravelled, and she dragged it through the wet sand until it could no longer serve its purpose. When she finally arrived at the picnic her father had set up, she had only her bucket and shovel, and she was too frustrated to play with either one.

That had been decades ago, but somehow she still felt as though she was dragging that wet towel on her way to a picnic she would never be able to sit and enjoy.

"Honey, I was right there ready to help you. All you had to do was ask," her father had said when she arrived in tears.

"All you have to do is ask," her patient reminded her every week. "Just ask God to take over whatever it is that's bothering you. And while you're at it, remind Him to send me on home."

And now here she is, almost a week later, and she still has no idea what to tell her patient when she sees him tomorrow. He will certainly ask – he always does. She could lie to him, keep him comfortable by telling him she talked to God about it. But she has limited interactions and hates to waste one in deceit. *Well*, she reasons, *I can pray tonight. It's just a matter of voicing some words. It can't be that hard to say a quick prayer.* Or even just think it as she brushes her teeth before bed.

"Oh, toothpaste!" she exclaims as she whirls back into the store, frustrated at the delay, but the toothpaste cannot wait.

As Rachel rushes back through the door, she passes a young boy, perhaps nine years old, talking excitedly with his father.

They're wearing matching jerseys, and the child is holding more tubes of blue paint than they could possibly use. She smiles inwardly at their excitement.

Family. Her grin slips. *All those dreams about our future and children falling away with every hour spent beside his bed, taking care of his every need —*

She refuses to let her mind go there. Those were the yesterdays, and there had been some good ones. But today, she struggles to consider the memories with thankfulness, to remind herself that today, too, is a gift. After a day of feeding tube incidents and bed pan accidents, she is ready to retreat.

Although she was supposed to see Jon Thomas again tonight, she decides to cancel after the chaos of her day. They were going to go for a walk in the park, but making conversation feels impossible tonight. Third dates are awkward anyway, and Rachel knows she makes them even more so. She doesn't have any real complaints about Jon Thomas, but she's not yet comfortable enough with him to relax. A few years ago, she thought she would never have to face another awkward date again, but here she is.

"Sorry about your fiancé," Jon Thomas had acknowledged after he introduced himself. "This must feel like a new world again, huh?"

"Why is that?"

"Well, just being back out on dates and stuff," Jon Thomas backpedalled. "Sorry, I don't know why I said that. Just trying to make conversation," he had admitted nervously before changing the subject. "So, um, what do you like to do in your spare time, like for fun?"

"Not a whole lot, honestly. The weekdays feel pretty busy. Sometimes I read, make plans for my patients, or walk my dog. What about you?"

"Oh cool, you've got a dog? What kind is it?"

"Cassie's a mutt. She looks like a shepherd-lab mix of some kind. Do you like dogs?" she ventured hopefully. She couldn't help but feel her heart reach out as it had so many years ago.

I actually prefer dog people myself. They tend to be loyal and don't mind a mess. Can I throw one –

"I guess I'd like them if I wasn't allergic," Jon Thomas's voice had plunged in to pull her back from the flood of memories. But in the happy wake of the daydream, it didn't feel like a rescue.

"Oh, you're allergic," she had repeated blankly. "Oh, that's too bad." She could not think of anything else to say, so he had changed the subject.

Keenly aware of just how short today falls in comparison to the life she had imagined back then, Rachel pulls out her phone to cancel with Jon Thomas. The exhausting conversations will have to wait for another day, and she decides to walk Cassie instead. Today she, like all people, simply needs love. And toothpaste.

11

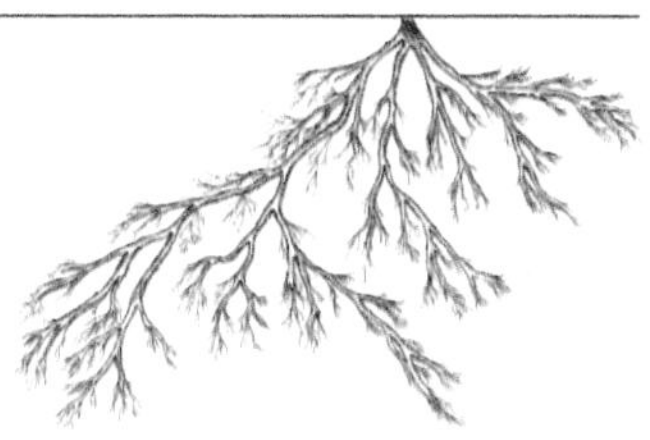

Face Paint

"Looks like fun," I say to the boy with his arms full of paint tubes. I have no idea what team they could be rooting for, or even which sport is currently in season, but I have to smile at his enthusiasm.

He looks up at me, his eyes bright with excitement. "If we win this one, we'll stay undefeated, and my dad says we can get milkshakes after! I'm going to get mint chocolate chip!"

"Well then, I hope you win," I offer, even though I can't stand mint chocolate chip ice cream. *It tastes like toothpaste with chunks of chocolate in it.*

The father laughs at his son's eagerness.

"Let's go, bud, we're going to be late. We already have way too much of this stuff, and I imagine we'll have more paint on us than the rest of the crowd put together."

"Well, they're all going to be wishing they looked like us when we win!" the boy argues happily. Jabbing his finger proudly into the air, he yells, "We're number one, and we're going to prove it tonight!" I smile as they walk away.

The boy bounds ahead as they head to the cash register to purchase their spoils. The father grabs a candy bar and slides it next to the tubes of paint on the conveyor belt. This is a big night − a very special guys night out – and they are not going to waste a single opportunity.

After paying the cashier and walking through the busy part of the parking lot, they break into a run, racing to their old black sedan. A painted "Happy Father's Day" proclamation runs sloppily across the back window in child's handwriting, the sentiment lingering even though it has been months since the holiday. When asked about it, the father feigns indifference about the appearance of his car, making excuses about why he hasn't had time to wash it. But, in reality, he has worked diligently to preserve his son's expression of love. *Enjoy it while you can,* he tells himself, *they say all kids outgrow their parents eventually.*

Of course, he had never outgrown his father. Maybe it was because he never felt the security to look his father in the eye, man to man. The footing between them had never been level enough for that. He had spent the better part of his life trying to catch his dad's eye and make him proud. But he had never quite been able to hold his father's attention.

"Dada, look," his shrill toddler voice had squealed every evening in their big front yard.

"Hey! Daddy, watch me," his five-year-old voice had begged every summer from the swing set.

"Hey, Dad! Hey! Dad, look what I can do," his eleven-year-old voice had called from his skateboard on the driveway.

"Dad, look, I think I might ask her to be my girlfriend," his thirteen-year-old voice had cracked as he pointed proudly at his school yearbook.

"Hey, Dad, call me back," his sixteen-year-old voice had pleaded as he tried to figure out why the car wouldn't start.

"Hi, Dad, this is Lisa," his twenty-one-year-old voice had trembled on his wedding day.

"Hey, Dad," he had whispered to the bare white wall as he held his own son in the hospital, "I won't ever be anything like you." Then he turned to the baby and teared up, "I will always love you, buddy. I'm your biggest fan right here. But don't tell your mom I said that."

"I can hear you," his wife said from across the room.

He glanced up. "Okay, we can both be his biggest fans." He was quiet for a minute, then admitted, "I have no idea how to be a dad. I mean, look at me, I could really, really do some damage. How will I not mess this up?"

Lisa smiled, "Because you're not the same man he was. You're kind, you're good. I mean, for one thing, you're here." They had often talked through his fears in the months leading up to their son's arrival, the same conversation playing out over and over. "Kids can be different from their parents. You can break the cycle. You're seeing it, and that's got to be the first step."

"I really hope you're right," he said. Turning back to his son, he whispered quietly, "I really hope she's right. And I promise you this, I'm going to try with all my heart."

Growing up, he had stood uncertainly at his father's side trying to earn his approval. His father had not been an abusive man or even an angry one. He was merely absent. There were no low lows just as there were no high highs – only a general sense of disinterest slathered over every interaction.

Living in the shade of his father's indifference had only reinforced his fear that he was somehow less than he should be. *If my own father would rather read the paper or watch the news, getting everyone else's opinion on any given topic, why would anyone else want to hear what I have to say?*

It undermined his courage as he offered himself to the world. He was always afraid that he was bothering his teachers, offending his peers, annoying his bosses. If his father had held the bottom of the ladder secure, he could have climbed confidently up to his place in the world. But his father's unsteady grip instead made the way uncertain, even if only in his perception of himself.

He had determined in the hospital that his own son would never feel that insecurity. *This kid is definitely going to outgrow me,* he smiled to himself, imagining the many ways his affection would annoy the boy as he grew. But he didn't care. *Better to be embarrassed of what you've got than to wonder why you don't have it*, he reasoned.

But for his eight-year-old son, that day has not yet come. They walk into the stadium, into the picture-perfect fruition of many months of planning. The magic flooding the young boy's mind overflows, and his father is caught up in the thrill.

And yet, events like this have a bittersweet edge to them – the simple satisfaction of being in the company of his son fills his soul with happiness, but it also stirs up his old insecurities. Events like these are a privilege of fatherhood, a perk rather than a begrudged responsibility.

"Hey buddy, watch this," he hears his thirty-year-old voice shout above the crowd as he throws a piece of popcorn high into the air and catches it in his mouth.

His son looks him in the eye and beams – it is just as cool as he thought it would be. Getting caught up in the excitement of the moment, his son suddenly screams wildly, joining the cheers for a team he loves simply because his father loves them, because he got a matching jersey for his birthday. His father smiles to see that the boy feels none of the loneliness with which he has been cursed; he hopes his son will never know what it is to not belong.

But no one hears the child. In a stadium where all sixty thousand people are talking at once, the chatter of a little boy fascinates only the one who brought him. The man smiles at his boy as they hurry up the stairs to find their seats. They are late to the game, but no one in the stadium will notice, crowds being a remarkably ironic place to lose oneself.

And they do lose themselves in the evening. Their team plays poorly through the first quarter, fumbling the ball and missing an easy field goal. The man and his son join the throng in expressing their disapproval – they yell at the team and boo the refs. But as the game progresses, their team comes from behind, gradually closing the gap with several plays worthy of the highlight reel. As the clock runs out, the entire stadium is on its feet, holding its breath and leaning to assist the final pass. A Hail Mary, it miraculously finds its mark in a sea of defenders to win the game. The crowd bursts into a frenzy.

He lifts his son high into the air and spins around before setting the dizzy boy back in his seat. He knows the celebration is absurd. Even as he high fives his son and the stranger sitting next to him, he longs to exchange the commotion of the stadium for the security of friendship with those who don't leave when the game is over.

Still, it feels good to win. And ice cream certainly never hurt anything. He pushes back his thoughts to enjoy the moment.

"So, milkshakes? We can stop at our favorite spot when we get closer to home." He turns to his son who can no longer contain the excitement of a win, an undefeated season, and a mint chocolate chip milkshake.

"I scream, you scream, we all scream for ice cream!" His son jumps, spins around, and bumps into a middle-aged lady wearing the same blue jersey.

"Oh, sorry," he says, slinking back toward his father.

"No, baby, we're celebrating that one! Oh wow, your face looks incredible," the lady exclaims, giving the boy a high five and smiling at his father. The man mouths his silent apologies and gratitude.

As they drive home, the boy relives all the exciting moments. Even after they stop for their milkshakes, he alternates between recounting each big play of the game and struggling to avoid brain freezes as he hurries through his treat. Nothing is lacking. *Is this what rest is,* the young dad wonders, *what it feels like when nothing is missing?* All the world is right as they drive home in the dark.

He glances back at his son's delighted face, getting lost in the moment.

"I'm so glad we finally got to do this today," he says. "I love hanging out with you."

"Me too," the boy agrees. "That was awesome."

"Dad!" his son screams, and his eyes flash back to the road as a dark figure blurs in front of his right headlight. The world slows, and he slams his brakes as a thud reverberates from the front side panel and a cloud of papers explodes into the air.

"What was that? Bud, are you okay? What was that?" he yells, swerving to a hasty stop on the side of the road. His locked seatbelt holds him fast, and he frantically struggles to free himself. "Are you okay?"

"Yeah. I lost my milkshake." The boy stares straight ahead. His treat drips down the back of the passenger seat and pools at his feet.

"Wait here, don't look back there."

The father leaps from the car and runs a few steps before his fears materialize in the silhouette of a crumpled human form.

"Oh God, oh help me. It's a person. Oh, help me."

He sprints back to the car and flings the door open.

"Hey, bud, where's my phone? Here, call 911. Don't look back, bud, look over here at me. I need you to call 911. Tell them someone's been hit by a car, and they need to come right away. We're, we're right in front of – what is this place? In front of the gas station, Dalton's Quick Stop."

The boy's eyes will not focus; instead he watches the ice cream, which drips from the seat to the floorboard at regular intervals. His mind is afraid to process what he thinks he has seen, and he cannot pull himself back to the moment.

12

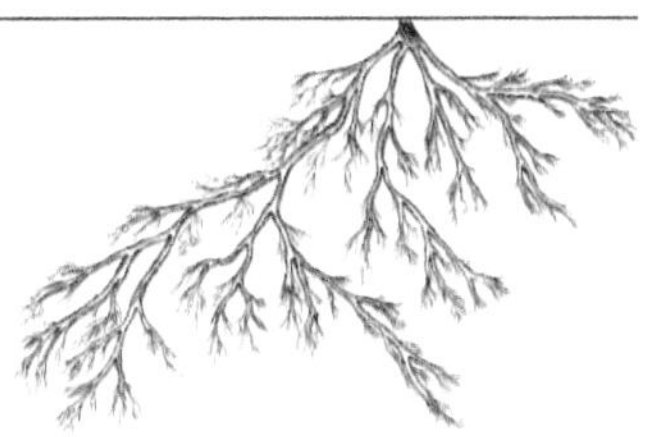

Respect

I snatch the phone from his paralyzed hands and order him again not to look as I race back to the motionless body. I call 911 and drop to my knees, listening for a breath, feeling for a pulse. The woman's wrist flops limp in my hand, the loose magazine pages swirl around us, the calm voice asks my location, the darkness fuels my hope that I am dreaming – *please, God, wake me from this nightmare. Please God, help me help her.*

I stay on the phone while I lean over the woman. As I begin chest compressions, unsure if I'm doing them right, a shaggy old man comes running from the direction of the gas station. He hobbles with rapid speed on an uncooperative leg and shouts, but I can't understand him. He reminds me of a large bird awkwardly trying to run while taking flight as he bears down on me, motioning with his hands as he barks commands at me expectantly. The sounds blur together and join the high-pitched ringing in my head as my mind withdraws.

The man gruffly grabs my shoulder and shoves me aside. He falls to his knees, tilts her head back, and leans an ear to her face. Then he begins the compressions again, far more vigorously than mine.

"Ruby!" he yells. "Hey, stay with me, Ms. Ruby! Ruby, it's Phil. Hey, stay with me now. Man, you call 911? Is that them on the phone?" he shouts quickly at me before turning back to the woman.

"Ruby, can you hear me?" He continues to count silently as he assumes the role of her heart.

"Yes, this is them," I offer, holding up my phone. "They're coming. They said, they would be, um…they say, they're on their way, that they, um…they're coming," I pick up his cap that has fallen aside during his efforts. I trace the embroidered yellow letters with my fingers and run my hand across the badge, a spectrum of flags.

"Listen, man, count these for me, okay?" He attempts to pull my focus back, to keep the shock from overtaking me completely. "Count off to thirty — okay, here's three…"

"Three, four, five…" I continue aimlessly, forgetting to stop at thirty. Lost, I set his hat back down and begin picking up the papers strewn about her, smoothing the crumpled sheets back into the worn folder I found near her face. By the time the flashing lights signal that help has arrived, I realize I have counted the pages rather than the compressions.

Rattled, I look back at the man – still working, still counting, still talking to her. The paramedics leap from the truck to take over for him.

"She's breathing!" The man shouts, still hovering beside them. "You stay with me, Ruby. I'm right here. That's right." He continues to talk to her, and they ask him to give them more space.

The police arrive and approach him with some questions. He directs them to me, points at my car. *My car. My boy!* I rush back to the car and find him curled up in the back seat. He looks up at me with red eyes.

"Dad? Are they dead?"

"No, bud – no, she's okay. They're taking her to the hospital to check her out, and they'll fix her up, but she's alive. She's okay – I think she may be okay." My boy starts to cry and can't stop, his fears and relief physically pouring from his small body. "I need to go answer a few questions now. Okay, bud? I'll be back in a few minutes. I'll be right back."

"Okay. Who is that old man?"

"I'm not sure. He must've been over at the gas station and seen it happen. I'm really glad he was here, though – I'm pretty sure he saved her life." We both glance in his direction, watching as he picks up his hat. He sets it on his head for a moment, pulls it down to wipe his forehead, then resettles it in its place.

The man was ready for a moment like this. Although his training was a lifetime ago, he has stood at attention, waiting for a reason to call upon it ever since.

As a teenager, he had enlisted with all the idealism of a man in his youth – his future stood primed and blank, a canvas awaiting its masterpiece. The training had made sense to him, that way of life falling obediently into place as he marched in community. The travel had astonished him, the beauty of a landscape he had never seen opening his mind to the immense design of a Creator. The combat had broken him, the nightmares snatching his sense of security as they reached for him in the dark. The return home had crippled him, his new reality resisting as he struggled to tuck it back into the crisp creases of a fashionable society which looked always forward, never back.

At first, his community took pity on him and strove to accommodate the wounded veteran needing a season to heal. When time didn't bring about the return of his grounded mind, they shifted nervously at his embittered comments and reckless lifestyle. As society rolled on to bigger freedoms and better opportunities, people rolled their eyes in annoyance at his refusal to ride along. The world completed its grieving process long before he was ready, and he was left behind.

"It's tough, Phil, but you just gotta find a way to get past it," his younger brother had told him one evening as they drove home from the bar. The kind owner had called Phil's family yet again to ask them to come and get him before he caused any more trouble.

"How? How do you just 'get past' it? How do you just go on living like everything's fine after what I've seen? Tell me, seriously, tell me, how a human being is supposed to get over something like that."

"Okay, okay, that was a bad choice of words. I don't know, man. But I saw stuff too," his brother pointedly reminded him. "You gotta figure something out though. I mean, there's people you can talk to, and I can even go with you. But I don't think you can just keep on like this."

"Yeah? Did you park in front of John Mill's house and try to pull yourself together, to man up enough so you could pass on his final words to his wife? And then she opens the door with his five-year-old kid right there and all you can do is cry? And next thing you know, she's falling apart again, sobbing into your shoulder, and you're the stranger in the front hall trying to tell her that it's going to be okay when you both know it's not? You know what that's like?"

He closed his eyes and shuddered, but the image remained.

"No, Phil, I sure don't," his brother admitted. "Sometimes the right words just aren't there – "

"I had the right words – John told me exactly what to say." Phil had rehearsed them as the doctor examined him, as he flew home, as he shined his boots, as he drove to the address on the paper.

And when she opened the door, the words disappeared.

And when she burst into tears, the only words that shook loose were the ones no one believed anyway.

"I mean, he had a wife and kid. What kind of God looks down at two guys on the front and takes the one with everything to lose?"

"I don't understand any of it, and I won't pretend to," his brother conceded. "But do you ever think this could be a second chance or something?"

Phil sneered but didn't say anything, so they sat in silence for a few minutes. Each stared out the windshield as the miles passed one after the other, marked in time only by the rhythmic passing of dotted lines beneath the dashboard.

"And look what I've made of myself," Phil said finally. "Done John and his boy real proud, huh?"

"Well it's not too late, Phil," his brother tried to turn the conversation. "It never is." Though both brothers immediately doubted his statement, neither said any more.

It had begun as a gradual fall down through the grid of society, each framework breaking under his weight as he leaned on it for support. Close friendships were allowed to expire. Courtesies granted to the hometown hero began to pass him the bill. His debts piled up with an aggression that inversely reflected his ability to cope with his return home. His desperate efforts to hold all things together continued to decline until he came home one evening to find an eviction notice posted on his door.

The idea of homelessness did not greatly bother him. He had options. He could seek shelter at the mission or promise his brother that he would get help in exchange for a place to stay. However, the simpler life appealed to Phil, and he found healing in it that he could never find when he was trying to keep up with societal norms. The people he met on the streets were beautiful, and they did not pretend to have their lives in order. Many had similar stories, and here, in this marginalized corner of society, he found a home.

"I'm actually only 'houseless,'" he liked to correct those who spoke of his living situation. "I've got people, so I got a home and everything I need."

Since the war had stolen any joy he could find in the world before, Phil resolved on his first evening under the stars to not only rediscover the beauty around him but to create it himself. Although the missions were menial, they brought him great pleasure.

A roadside game he particularly liked to play was one he called "The Righting of the Hubcaps." As he walked along, Phil would scan the side of the road for hubcaps that had come loose and rolled away. Whenever he found one hiding in the grass, he picked it up and set it upright along the curb or against a sign post.

On the one hand, he enjoyed that they looked like smiling faces when he arranged them that way. On the other hand, someone might come looking for them, and hubcaps were much easier to spot sitting up like that. In addition to making Phil happy, The Righting of the Hubcaps also touched the hearts of the people who had long ago withdrawn their favor from him.

As the people drove by, they smiled out their windows at the standing hubcaps, which reinforced their senses of order and security.

"Must be the city making sure we can find our property if we lose something," one said. The other passengers nodded. Indeed, they did live in a nice city.

As the people turned, they scowled out their windows at the unkempt man hobbling aimlessly along the other side of the road.

"Must be some addict looking for something of value so he can fund his habit," one said. The other passengers agreed. Indeed, the growing homeless population threatened the order and security of their city.

That was the thing about homelessness – people forgot Phil was human. Regardless of whether they thought he was an addict, a convict, or a lunatic, they rarely spoke to him. They mostly looked away while they walked past him, as though he was invisible. Or they placed a hand on their purses, as though he was out to take what was theirs. Or they clutched their children close, as though he was out to hurt them. Or they handed him money without even a word, as though he was less than a man.

But tonight, under the flash of the lights, they marvel at his ability to handle the situation and congratulate him on a life saved, a job well done. They address him with the respect he cannot hope to receive when he walks along the road.

"Excuse me, sir, could I ask you a couple of questions?"

"When you're finished, sir, could you please step over here so she can take your statement?"

He finishes answering their questions and walks over to the father and son huddling together by their car, the "Happy Fathers Day" message a dark irony under the flashing lights.

"You did good – I saw you got all her papers together," Phil says graciously and shakes hands with the trembling man sitting on the curb. "Don't know why, but those papers are the most important thing Ms. Ruby has. She'll be happy to see those – pretty sure you got every one of 'em."

The younger man smiles and shakes his head, seen as a man by a man for the first time in his life. He would say more, but he doesn't want to break down in front of his son.

The older man nods back at him and turns to walk slowly across the street, his mind mulling over the words of a song he often hears downtown late at night. That catchy one with the strange name, something about a Mr. Arnold, with the chorus that goes like this:

> *My eye sinks inward and your heart lies plain,*
> *All these unspoken words between us we keep sayin'*
> *And what we mean, we say,*
> *And what we would, we know*
> *Concrete cracks where the flower grows.*

Humming the song, the old man limps back to his place under the overhang of the convenience store, dropping into his makeshift bed fashioned from blankets and newspapers. He pulls his backpack closer and rifles through it until he finds his water bottle and takes a sip. Heart still racing, he settles himself back and closes his eyes for a moment before opening his book again, unaware of the silent prayers rising from his lips.

Epilogue

If I can't be a river. Those are the words he had used, and though I agreed, they had picked at a loose thread on the fringe of my mind. This is an overwhelming city, one of those places in which people see through each other as they pass from one activity to the next. If they did pause, they might find something amazing here, some mesmerizing lunge at the soul, that both swells like stringed music and haunts like the dark of a lonely road.

They analyze our amazing architecture and unfettered dreams. They coast past our luxurious homes and glance at our freshly-groomed dogs beside our shiny cars parked in the drive. They look but never see the people who live in these homes and love these dogs and wax these cars because they are the best friends we have.

Although hopeful, his words had voiced a twinge of the homesickness that falls heavily on the far side of an ever-revolving heart. I know he has seen far more of the world than I have, but against the backdrop of this city that threatens to swallow us whole, we are all raindrops – small drips on the windshield that are quickly swished away.

As I helped him pack all of his belongings into his shopping cart, I handed him his blanket that reeked of mildew. He's a regular outside the store, and we don't mind him sitting out here as long as the customers don't mind. But when his presence makes them uncomfortable, it's my job to ask him to move along, so our conversation had started out like most of them do when I'm wearing my red vest and name tag.

"Hey, Greg," I said. "You doing okay today?"

"Yeah, sure am. Thanks," he replied. "Guess you got a complaint already today," he said, shaking his head. "You're from around here, aren't you?"

When I nodded, he told me the city sounds just like it did when he was a child, living in a tall building tucked in the heart of New York City.

It was a simple apartment, a dingy little place with two small beds jutting out into the living space between the kitchen and the bathroom. Then city planners came in and decided to revamp the area, so the little apartment on a dirty street was now sitting in a glamorous little location surrounded by the rich and famous.

In the wintertime when their parents let them head down to the park, the children used to walk the paths looking for treasures or toys they had hidden during the summer. They would play "leap the landscaping" where it got so narrow they could bound right across to the other side. They built pretend fires and ate raw marshmallows and crammed too many people into that little apartment for Christmas. But the place never ran out of room – it just kept giving way and giving more.

"That deep red carpet hid every stain we ever made," he laughed, remembering the days that he fastened his cape and adventured with his brothers and sister across the floor of the apartment without touching the carpet. The little ruffians always trusted their endless supply of pillows to hold them for one more step. It never did, and they never learned, and life was good.

And in the summers, they walked across the street and picked flowers in front of the office building on the other side – proof they had made it across. Those pressed flowers still mark the pages of old books in his sister's house.

"You can't do that now, with all the suits and crazy folks. You'd get run over. But man, that place back in the day…" And he sighed with longing, yearning for the moment of time as much as the place itself. But places are the keepers of memory, the closest we can get to recovering the good old days. He pines for the little apartment, but mostly for its ability to preserve the happy days of his childhood.

But now, that momentary snapshot doesn't exist any more. The apartment itself still stands, but that spot in his heart does not. Sure, if he looks out the wide windows, he can still see the sparkling lights of the skyline. And stepping out on the narrow balcony at the summer's end, he can still hear the bustle of the traffic rushing below as autumn approaches.

"But it's not the same, either," he tried to explain. "Because generations of voices who narrated the family videos have passed on. And you pull out your phone to try to capture the memories, to take up that mantle, but your voice is just too weak to give them their proper weight. I went back to see it again a few weeks ago, and everything's the same and nothing is."

That stubborn red carpet still hides all the stains. Those pillows still create paths for little feet to scamper across floors of lava, children reaching down to scoop up handfuls of the volcanic ash for imaginary facials. But now, even though other children are jumping over the lava and running through the park and doing gymnastics on the bed, his soul is the one that is just so tired.

He has experienced griefs that have wrenched his heart and threatened his faith, that have shaken the solid ground he took for granted. And running down the back alley to the flower patch and finding it paved over with a dumpster on top only served to remind him of the things he has lost.

"Or maybe the things I've found," he mused, "I'm not sure. Because I used to think that if I could just get to the place, I'd be back in that fortress of childhood innocence, where life waited for me while I took my time. And then to walk through the place a few weeks back and to see the sad people in the city park, and the bright

LED lights, and the dumpster over the flower patch – it almost looks like progress, but it feels like pain. This isn't how things were, and yet here they are."

The flower patches continue to dissolve to make way for more initiatives, even as he gathers the fragile petals with his memories and struggles to fashion them into the bookmarks he used to flatten with the iron. Pounding, pressing, trying to make things be the way they were, stay the way they were…but unable to return to that place once again.

"You ever hear of Emily Dickinson?" he had asked. "She wrote poems back in the 1800s or so."

I shrugged and said I thought I had. I don't like poetry, but I think I had to read her work while I was in school.

"Before my mom passed away, she recited one line of hers that's always stayed with me. Anyway it goes, 'That it will never come again is what makes life so sweet.' It seems to get truer as I get older."

He told me he regrets taking it all for granted back then. He wishes he had spent a few more nights sitting on the balcony, listening to the laughter across the way as voices echoed back and forth between the tall buildings. He wishes he had spent a few more afternoons on that fire escape, just observing. He wishes he had worked with his mom in the kitchen more and not just eaten his meals there.

"Maybe," he said, "I just wish I'd put that whole apartment and those days in a juicer and just pressed and squeezed and kept right on squeezing. That was the world back then, and I figured it'd always be like that – just 'keep on keeping on,' like my granddad always said."

I had nodded with a knowing smile. My granddad used to say that, too. I picked up a magazine as I helped him pack up his stuff, but the cover tore, and it slipped from my grasp before falling to the ground. I apologized as I stooped to pick it up.

"Nah, that's alright," he waved me aside, deep in his own thoughts. "I don't know, it was just a simpler time. I mean, we got dirty in those grimy city streets, but it all washed out at the end of the day. Or you just wore those clothes anyway."

"Yeah, I know what you mean," I said, letting the conversation lapse. He glanced down the street and opened his mouth to speak but changed his mind. I handed him his backpack, the last of his things.

"I'll say this, and then I'll let you get back to it – " he began.

"No rush," I interrupted, checking my watch, "I've got another four and a half hours." *Plus, sometimes it's nice to meet another human.*

"Well, then I'll just say – I sometimes feel like life's just hurtling by, and I'm afraid that I'll never be able to just stop and make something meaningful of my life, you know? As I've wandered, it's started me thinking that if I could choose, I'd want to be more like a river, carving my way into that landscape. People wouldn't have any doubt that I'd been here, that I'd changed my world in some way – you know, hopefully for the good."

"Yeah," I said. I wasn't sure exactly where he was going, but I tried to follow along.

He glanced down before continuing, "But maybe God's check on the human ego is that He makes us raindrops instead of rivers." Although he looked straight into my eyes, his gaze ran past me and lodged much deeper into himself. I wondered if maybe he had been beaten down by more than one river as a younger man. "I mean, you admire the things because they're so impressive, but left unchecked they destroy a lot of beautiful things as they rage through."

He loaded his backpack onto the cart, patting the handle twice as if to signal that he had reached the end of his thoughts. As he shook my hand, he concluded – finally presenting what, I believe, he had been trying to put into words all along.

"And so I'm a raindrop," he said, and he turned to meet my eyes again, seeing me this time. "But if that's what I have to be, then I want to be a raindrop in the sand. I don't want to be another drop in the ocean, a drip in the bucket, just a quick splash into the puddle of what has already been. At least in the sand, I've moved something, changed something, maybe even left a little something of myself behind....You know, if I can't be a river."

And I do, I know exactly what he means.

But I also know he walks slowly, and I know where we keep the blankets. If I hurry, I can catch him.

Acknowledgments

With heartfelt thanks...

To Ian, for encouraging me at every step. You have rescued me from many mistakes (in writing and life) with humor and grace – thank you for creating a safe place where we can laugh together. I appreciate your keen eye for accuracy and inconsistencies. This story is better because of you, and so am I. You are a gift.

To Mom and Dad, for your unwavering support throughout the writing of this book. Thank you for your enthusiasm for the story when it was a rough idea and for your insight into the characters. Many of them reflect your wisdom as you've shared it with me, and I am forever grateful to have been born into your family, to see your love for our Father firsthand. You are a gift.

To Aunt Sharon, for encouraging me to write about beautiful things. At a critical point in my life, you showed me that stories can be true and beautiful, that art doesn't have to be cynical to be true. Thank you for your encouragement, as well as your honest and careful feedback that made this book better, more true. You are a gift.

To Kim, for putting your heart into many readings of manuscripts and offering your insight to make them better. This story is clearer because of your thoughtfulness. It seems you have a knack for helping books, as well as people, become the best versions of themselves. Thank you for caring about this book like it was your own. You are a gift.

To Kara, for your belief in this story and your desire to see it published. Your excitement for this book has been the wind in my sails many times throughout this process. Thank you for your willingness to offer suggestions and even characters to make the book a better reflection of our world. Your friendship and your wisdom mean so much. You are a gift.

To Lauren, for your friendship in all of life and your dedication to the strict "No talking, but definitely Cheesecake Factory" rule on our work trips. Thank you for your feedback and encouragement during my frustration while building out shaky new characters – you helped me to stay the course. You are a gift.

To Millie, for taking time (in the midst of a crazy schedule) to read through my ever-changing manuscripts. Your wisdom as a writer and, more importantly, as a friend have been a continuous blessing since that random placement freshman year. I am who I am today because of your friendship. You are a gift.

To Brittney, for taking the time to read and offer helpful observations. Your thoughtful suggestions have made the characters more believable, and your advice to "write what you know" was invaluable in forming some of the more difficult characters. You are a gift.

To Laura, for jumpstarting this book by issuing the challenge to start writing and cheering me on even with my slow start. You are a gift.

To the number of other friends who have encouraged me at each step of the process, for your prayers, wisdom, feedback, and support. You guys are a gift.

And to God, for your amazing love, seeking me out in ways I would not always have chosen in your relentless pursuit of my heart. This is your tale, just as all of our stories are part of your story. I pray I've told it well and that you use it to teach us all. You are the Giver of all good gifts.

About the Author

DEVON DIAL lives outside of Huntsville, Alabama with her husband and two children. She pursued a degree in English Literature while attending Bryan College before graduating from the University of Alabama in Huntsville with a Bachelor's Degree in Art Studio.

To contact Devon, please email her:
NeverAMereMortal@gmail.com